.

BENBECULA

A note on the author

Graeme Macrae Burnet is the author of five novels: the Booker-shortlisted *His Bloody Project*, which has been published in over twenty languages; the Booker-longlisted *Case Study* (named as one of the *New York Times'* 100 Notable Books of 2022); and the Georges Gorski trilogy, comprising *The Disappearance of Adèle Bedeau*, *The Accident on the A35* and *A Case of Matricide*. Graeme was born in Kilmarnock and now lives in Glasgow.

First published in hardback in Great Britain in 2025 by Polygon,
an imprint of Birlinn Ltd.

Birlinn Ltd
West Newington House
10 Newington Road
Edinburgh
EH9 1QS

www.polygonbooks.co.uk

1

ISBN 978 1 84697 731 2
eBook ISBN 978 1 78885 847 2

Typeset by 3btype, Edinburgh

MIX
Paper | Supporting
responsible forestry
FSC® C018072
FSC
www.fsc.org

Printed and bound in Great Britain by Clays Ltd, Elcograf S.p.A

BENBECULA

Graeme Macrae Burnet

It is dark now and my window onto the world is a small one. I do not know how much longer I will be here.

My name is Malcolm MacPhee. If you're wondering why it falls to me to tell this tale, it is for no other reason than this – I am the only one left.

Since the incidents I am to recount, my sister Marion and my brother John have also departed this place. I did not want them to go but nor could I blame them for wishing to leave. There is nothing here for our generation. Our way of life is dying but for the MacPhees of Liniclate it came to a more abrupt end than for most. This for on the ninth day of July 1857 my brother Angus did to death my father, my mother and my aunt, all in the most brutal and purposeful fashion.

There may be some among you who know as little of Benbecula as I do of the great townships of Stornoway or Portree. There is not much to say. We are an island and a small one at that. The land is flat and sodden. I have been a few times to Lochmaddy on the Uist to the north but no further. I know there is more to the world than the stretch of shore between Creagorry and Borve, but this is the world I know. Before the events I am to describe our family grew what crops we could and gathered seaware for kelp. More enterprising folk than us abandoned this trade long before I was expelled from my mother's womb, and if we persisted in it, it was not for the riches to be earned

– there is barely a shilling in it – but because we knew nothing else.

Such acts as my brother committed are not commonplace in our corner of the world and the stench of it lingers as the reek cleaves to the thatch. In a similar way, the madness that afflicted my brother attaches itself to his kin. The potato blight, as folk round here are wont to say, does not affect a single plant. The whole crop is destroyed.

Thus I see few people these days. Mrs MacLeod visits weekly and now and again the priest MacGregor, though I fear he has given up on me as I have given up on him. I have no appetite to till and sow, and the place is going to ruin. Children take the long way round, along the shore path at the foot of the croft. They call this the Murder House and think me a madman, as if it was me rather than my brother who did to death half its occupants. I am sometimes given to wondering if I have in fact become what they think me to be but I believe I remain in possession of my reason.

In happier times our family consisted of myself, my father, my mother, my three siblings and aunt – that is my father's sister – who lived in a smaller dwelling a few yards behind our own and took most of her meals with us. Though they were not related by blood, my mother and my aunt were of such similar physical type, being likewise squat, big-bosomed and wide in the hip, that they were often taken to be twins. If it had been my father's intention to seek the image of his sister when he took a wife he could have done no better. The weather in these parts is harsh. Throughout the black months our island is lashed with rain and gales blow continually off the sea. Women of my mother and aunt's type are as well adapted to this climate here as the black-faced sheep that seem oblivious to the elements. They were ill-natured women and their conversation consisted mainly of plaints about their circumstances and the denigration of our neighbours. My father was taller and lean in the face and body. When not anchored by a cas-chrom or flaughter you might fear the wind would carry him off. And feeble as he was in body he was likewise in character, being placid and biddable. I never heard him raise his voice in anger and he met good and ill fortune with the same apathy. Had he had the opportunity to be informed of his death at the hands of his own son, he would likely have replied, Ach, these things happen.

Of we four siblings Marion was the eldest and best, and it is her removal from this place that pains me most. She herited not from my mother's side but my father's, being slender and long-faced. She was strong and never one to shirk labour more fitted to men but there was a solemnity about her. Laughter did not come readily to her lips and she appeared to take more satisfaction in the service of others than in her own pleasure. Of John, the youngest, there is little to be said. He was my father's replica in character but more simple-minded. He was not work-shy but required constant supervision and praise. We were none of us MacPhees greatly educated but John was incapable of learning anything. If he one day dropped a stone on his foot, he would the next day drop another stone on his foot and treat the pain he experienced with the same idiotic surprise. He was neither melancholy nor cheerful, and if there was ever a gathering of some sort it was difficult to recall if he had been present or not. Unless John takes it upon himself to procreate – and I fear he has not the wherewithal – I will be the last of the MacPhees of Liniclate. That is no bad thing. It is a poisoned lineage and no one round here shall lament our extinction.

Which brings us to the individual this narrative most concerns and who bears responsibility for my solitary existence. Angus was from the beginning quite singular. From the moment he could walk, he was never still. He would tear around the house upsetting whatever objects were set upon the table, unmoved by our mother's reprimands. She often grabbed and slapped him mercilessly but this had no effect. Outside he would chase after livestock which greatly antagonised our neighbours. I do not think he intended any harm to the beasts he chased. Rather I think he was simply in thrall to his own impact on the world. As a child he continually indulged in pranks and would laugh uncontrollably if someone tripped on a wire he had set or was soaked by a pail of water he had balanced above a door. The beatings such transgressions earned him were no deterrent. Angus was never cowed by authority, whether that of the priest, his teachers or the ground officers who were on his account frequent visitors to our house. Despite this, there was something endearing about him. His laughter infected people even as they chastised him and he had a way of looking contrite and then casting up his eyes and smiling that disarmed even those who sought his punishment. On account of the five years which separated us we were not close. I did not enjoy the attention he attracted and would take myself as far from him as possible. As a result I acquired a reputation of being truculent and aloof and it may be true that I was what people supposed me to be. It was only when Angus reached the age at which certain changes visit the body that he became properly troublesome. Certain traits that may be excused in a child are less easily forgiven in a man. From the moment he grew hair on his balls Angus had a shameless fascination for those parts of his body and their functions that decency normally dictates are kept private. Perhaps on account of his degenerate habits, he ceased to grow beyond the age of fourteen or so. He was squat like our mother, but barrel-chested and powerful. When he moved across the landscape, he seemed to do so with preternatural speed. There was also something hideous in his demeanour. He had no nameable deformity, yet even those encountering him for the first spurned him. By this time I would be gathering seaware, hard at work on the rig or sometimes labouring for a few shillings on the dykes and tracks of the parish. Through this industry, I sought to differentiate myself from Angus, yet I was haunted by the sense that I was not his opposite but his mirror image.

Some weeks prior to the murders, Angus was sent to labour at the house of Lachlan MacPherson at Lochdhar across the sound on the Uist to the south. I had previously been in service to MacPherson and found him to be a high-handed and pernickety individual. He is a shoemaker, and by virtue of this profession and the fine house in which he dwells he thought himself superior to me and to the others in his employ. He would frequently find fault with the execution of the most menial chores and would set myself and others to useless tasks for no other purpose than to lord it over his minions. He could not bear to see a person idle. Once when he discovered me in the crime of pausing for a smoke at the back of an outhouse he confronted me with the words, Is it for the smoking of a pipe that I am paying you, MacPhee? I made no response as the answer to his question was self-evident. He was standing closer to me than was necessary and we each of us looked into the eyes of the other. I continued to suck on my pipe and it was my impression that he was contemplating what action he might take. I fully expected him to take the pipe from my mouth and dash it to the ground, and indeed I saw him do so in my mind's eye and had begun to contemplate in turn what my response would be to this action of his. He did not do so however and instead muttered that I should get on with my work and that he had his eye on me. There is no place for Sloth at Lochdhar, he said, nor for those who practise it. That evening when the servants sat down to eat, I was served a bowl of sowens while the others had mutton. None of them dared to give a share of their meal to me. I would have done no differently in their place but the discrepancy in our fare shamed us all and the meal was passed in silence. There were other similarly vexatious incidents and I took my leave before the expiration of my term of employment, telling MacPherson that I would send my brother in my stead, this on account of the fact that our family could not afford to forfeit any income no matter how irksome the means of earning it. I confess this act contained a grain of mischief on my part as there was not a fellow in the entirety of Benbecula more dedicated to the practice of Sloth than Angus.

I believe it was a Saturday that Angus returned from Lochdhar as on this day there tended to be larger numbers of folk fording the sound. There had been no communication during the time that he had been away, but as the fortnight for which he had been engaged had passed we were expecting his return. The channel between our island and that to the south is fordable only at low tide and on the day in question this occurred towards the end of the forenoon. John, Marion and I were at work on the shore. My father was pottering on the rig. From the shore one can see a mile or so in the direction of Creagorry. Even at that distance it was clear as soon as Angus made his appearance that some-thing was awry. He was not alone, but among a small crowd of people. In itself this was not unusual due to the dependence on the tide but there was something curious about the cluster of people who made their way towards Liniclate. Rather than spreading out and moving at their own pace, the crowd was gathered around a single individual. This individual was Angus, recognisable due to his stocky build and unruly hair. Even as a child he had a strong aversion to having his hair cut and would struggle violently whenever our mother attempted to do so. As the throng grew nearer, I could see that he was moving with an awkward gait, lurching from side to side and flapping his arms as if trying to fend off some unseen predator. Some-times a child would break from the loose circle and dash towards him as if provoking an injured animal. This caused Angus to gesticulate more wildly and rush at the child in question who would take refuge behind the skirts of its mother. Without discussion my siblings and I laid down our tools and set off along the shore path. As we approached the multitude, it became clear that Angus was in a violent temper and the game the children were playing with him was not in jest. The taunting of our brother ceased as we grew nearer, and once at a distance of a few yards all present came to a halt. It fell to me to take charge of the situation. It did not seem prudent to scold the crowd for ill-using him so I thought it best to make light of the situation.

Have they been filling you with whisky at Lochdhar, Brother?

Though his gaze was trained in my direction, Angus did not seem to recognise me and made no response.

It's a bit early in the day to be so full of whisky, I said.

I stepped towards him and grasped him by the elbow and said that we had best be getting him home. There was no smell of whisky on him.

He shook me off. Not expecting this, I took a step or two backwards. John looked to me for some instruction. If Angus had always been ungovernable, John was too much his opposite. The boy would not do up his bootlaces unless directed to do so. It was instead Marion who stepped between us.

You'll be ready for a bowl of soup, Angus, she said in a soothing voice.

I am not wanting any soup, he replied. Then he turned to me and grasped the lapel of my jacket. Give me some tobacco, he said. I've not had a scrap of tobacco these last days.

I told him he could have a smoke when we were back at the house.

Are you keeping your tobacco up your arse now? he said, and as he did so he grabbed my hair with his free hand and wrenched my head downwards. There had always been some rough and tumble between us, as is customary between brothers, but this was of a different nature. There was a violence in his actions that I had not known before. I was thrown off balance and found myself on my knees. Angus fell upon me and started to lay blows into my midriff, all the time making a dreadful snorting noise. There was some laughter from the onlookers. Marion took it upon herself to free me, clambering onto Angus's back. He then caught her a heavy blow across the mouth with his elbow and she was propelled some yards back onto her behind. I took the opportunity to wrest myself free of Angus's grip and threw myself upon him. At this point the laughter around us subsided and our neighbours MacSween and Munro came to my assistance. The three of us sat on Angus for some minutes. When he seemed to have been subdued we loosed our grip but he immediately started to flail his limbs and howl like a lunatic and it was decided that it would be necessary to tie him. I sent my brother John, who had thus far done no more than stand witness to the unfolding spectacle, to fetch some rope.

It took MacSween, Munro and myself some minutes to secure my brother's hands. We then bound his arms tightly to his sides and hauled him to his feet. There is a good weight to him and this was no small task. I prompted Angus to move with the toe of my boot and he allowed his legs to give way beneath him and fell once again to the ground. It was only at this point that I became properly enraged. Until then I had been caught up in the moment but it now struck me that there was something dissembling in my brother's behaviour. When we were very young Angus had a great dislike of attending school. From the earliest age he was wilful and did not like to be confined whether to the schoolroom or to any task that demanded concentration. It was the custom for the youngest pupils to sit at the front of the class and on one occasion I saw Angus begin to sway back and forth on his stool. He then began to moan like a swarm of bees and this caused the teacher Miss Gilchrist to stop writing on the blackboard and ask what was the matter. Angus did not reply but started to sway more violently. Miss Gilchrist grabbed his arms and rapped his knuckles with her ruler. Angus then got to his feet and spouting some gibberish began to run recklessly round the perimeter of the room. The other children greatly enjoyed this silly performance and began to laugh and clap their hands. Angus reached the front of the class and clambered onto Miss Gilchrist's desk and commenced to dance a mad jig. The teacher was a young woman not from these parts and had not the wherewithal to bring him down, so it fell to me to drag him from the table before he was thrown out of the room. He thus learned that by acting the buffoon he could get his own way. My parents did not care much for the education of their children. As they could neither read nor write themselves they saw no utility in it. You can't turn over the soil with a book, my father was wont to say.

Angus's behaviour now struck me as similarly devious but what purpose he might have, other than to humiliate his family in the eyes of our neighbours, was obscure to me. It was with no small difficulty that we dragged him the half-mile or so to the house and there we tethered him to the bed by his four limbs. After our neighbours had left, he kept up his revolt against the ropes and it was only after some hours that he exhausted himself and fell asleep. I sat through the night with him fearing that he might wake and do some injury to himself. At some point I must also have fallen asleep but I did so fitfully. In the morning Angus seemed calm and in the presence of my mother and father I went to untie his legs whereupon he immediately resumed his violent thrashing. It was only then that I began to think that his behaviour was not some mysterious ploy but that he might be afflicted by some sort of madness.

His condition remained the same for three days. He would not take any food and cursed the lot of us violently. On the fourth day he became less agitated. He spoke more sensibly and took a little porridge fed to him like an infant. When we loosened his tethers he did not writhe or kick out. Once completely untied he hauled himself to a sitting position and looked to all intents like a man waking from a heavy slumber. He behaved as if nothing amiss had occurred. Later that evening I accompanied him outside and we shared a pipe on the bench outside the house. It was a clement evening and the water on the sound was motionless. I asked him what had happened at Lochdhar.

At Lochdhar? he replied, as if the name meant nothing to him.

While you were working at the house of Lachlan MacPherson, I said. Something must have happened as you have been quite tormented since your return.

He looked at me and I saw that either I was wrong in my presumption that some incident must have caused this change in his behaviour or that he had simply no recollection of it.

During these days Marion kept her distance from Angus and refused to minister to him in any way. I could not blame her. The blow he had dealt her had knocked out two of her teeth and left the right side of her face swollen. Even as a girl she had not been blessed with fair looks and being the eldest of us all she had long since given up any hope of marriage. We MacPhees were all of us somewhat wedded to each other. Marion had in any case never been well-disposed towards Angus. She was a hard worker and took on more than her share of the daily round, no doubt to demonstrate that she was the equal or better of any man. Angus on the other hand had always been a shameless hummocker and used any pretext to avoid work. Perhaps wishing to induce some pang of guilt in him, Marion would wordlessly take up any chore he left undone but this only had the effect of convincing Angus that there was no necessity for him to do anything other than suck on his pipe. If I suggested some task to him, his customary reply was, Marion will do it.

Perhaps on account of our proximity in age, Marion

and I enjoyed a certain closeness, though not to the extent
of lying together. As youngsters we tended to the needs of
our younger siblings and in later years this mollycoddling
persisted, allowing both Angus and John to remain child-
like in their behaviour. I sometimes had cause to wonder if
it was me that was responsible for Angus's indolence.
Perhaps if I had administered him a good beating after the
incident in the schoolroom he would have changed his
ways. Certainly such a beating would never be forthcoming
from my father as for some unfathomable reason he had a
special affection for his third child. Our mother in contrast
could be quite vicious and on occasion engaged in hair-
pulling and other acts of petty violence. From a young age
however Angus was unnaturally strong and would return
whatever blows he received with equal force and after a
while she desisted.

A few days after his return from Lochdhar, we allowed
Angus to go at large. In the morning I would set him to
some task but he would soon let whatever tool he was
holding drop from his hand and wander off to the moors
behind the house. He would sit gazing towards the water
or lie back in the heather so that he was quite hidden, with
only the smoke from his pipe betraying his whereabouts.
I had neither the time nor inclination to constantly cajole
him. It was May. There was always work to be done and
less was accomplished if I wasted my time haranguing him.
It was easier all round to let him alone.

I do not know how old I am. Nor do I know what year I was born or what year it is now. The passage of time here is marked not by numbers but by the rhythm of the tides, the waxing and waning of the moon and the changing of the seasons. Also I suppose by the creaking in my bones and the failing of my mind. The man who took my statement after Angus committed his deeds wrote down that I was about thirty years of age. I know that the murders took place in the year of 1857 because the date was much repeated at the time, but I cannot say how many years have passed since then. Three or four perhaps. Or maybe it is more. I expect if I applied my mind to it, I could work it out but it makes no difference. Certainly I am not an old man. My age is roughly thirty plus however many years have passed since Angus's acts. When he had taken my statement at the Creagorry Inn where he had made his headquarters, the writer read it back to me and asked me to sign my name. The words he read to me were not really mine but his. I could not say with any certainty that everything had happened precisely the way I described it. It was not that I lied. I had no reason to lie just as I have no reason to lie now but there were moments when my memory failed me and I said things merely to give him something to write. He had come all the way from

Inverness, this man, and I did not want to disappoint him. All the same when he passed me his pen I made a cross at the foot of the page. I felt ashamed that I was no longer able to sign my name.

Since I have been alone – that is since Marion and John also departed this place – Mrs MacLeod comes once a week. Previously others came but for one reason or another, none of them persisted. Mrs MacLeod is here now. She asks how I am today.

How am I? This is a question I have difficulty answering. I am precisely as I am every day, having been brought into being because my parents' groins came together at a particular time and the egg and the ejaculate formed a foetus which grew in my mother's womb and became me. If that had not happened I would not have come into being. Had it happened at a different moment it would not have been me that was brought into existence but another person. Or perhaps – I am not sure on this point – it would have been an older or younger version of me. In any case, this is how I am and there is no variation in it from one day to the next. But I do not say any of this to Mrs MacLeod. Instead I tell her that I am quite well and enquire in turn how she is. She makes no reference to her parents' groins in her reply.

I'll be all the better when we have taken care of the business in hand, she says.

The business she is referring to is my monthly bath, this

being another of the ways in which I mark time. Previously
I would protest that I have no need of bathing but Mrs
MacLeod is unyielding on this point and it is less trouble
not to resist. She has already cleared the bottles and dishes
from the table and swept the floor. There is nothing to
stop me sweeping my own floor but sweeping is woman's
work, and despite my abject circumstances I have my pride
and it does not pain me to sit in my own stoor. In addition,
watching Mrs MacLeod sweep the floor brings me a
certain pleasure and were I to sweep my own floor I would
be deprived of this.

Mrs MacLeod now fills and sets the large pail over the
fire. She drags the tin bath to the centre of the room from
the corner in which it resides. It is not yet time for me to
disrobe so I sit on the bench at the table. She is my age or
a little older. I know this because we attended school
together. I did not attend long but she is one of those in the
parish to whom letters are taken to be read aloud or
dictated or who reads out directives issued by the factor.
She is an Educated Woman. She is also a handsome
woman. As a girl she was as slender as grass and seemed to
bend as she walked in the wind but labour and child-
bearing have thickened her hips and added heft to her
bosom. There is more of her to get your hands on but I have
never lain a finger upon her, and this not only for fear of a
punch on the jaw from Duncan MacLeod, who is a brawny
fellow with meaty fists. While the water warms she busies

herself returning various items to their proper places and I watch, my chin cupped in the palms of my hands.

She takes the scissors from a drawer and approaches me. I sit up and she gently pushes my forehead back so that my chin points upwards. She starts snipping at my beard. My face is inches from her chest.

She asks me if I have been at the whisky.

Why would I not have been at the whisky? I reply. These days I am always at the whisky. I can think of no reason not to be at the whisky.

My beard is matted and wiry and the scissors are blunt but I do not flinch.

She pauses and stands back to survey her work.

Better, she says.

She then places her hand on the back of my head and guides it forward. She snips at the hair around my ears and neck, all the time adjusting the position of my head with the tips of her fingers. I feel a stirring in my breeches. This cutting of the hair and beard is not a regular event. It does not take place every time I am made to take a bath. The cutting of my hair is less frequent than my bathing. It may even be that my bathing does not take place monthly but is more frequent or less frequent than that as I have no way of enumerating the passing of the weeks other than through the ritual of taking a bath. It is an assumption on my part that Mrs MacLeod is making me bathe because four weeks have passed but that may not be so. It may be

that only three weeks have passed and she is making me
bathe because I reek more than usual. Or perhaps five or
six weeks have passed and the frequency of my baths is
determined neither by the calendar nor by the intensity of
my odour but simply by her whim. In any case, it is
unusual for the cutting of the hair and the taking of the bath
to coincide.

Once four pailfuls of water have been poured into the
bath I set about undressing. This I do slowly for it is only
when five pailfuls have been added that I will step into the
water and there is no sense standing naked in the chamber
for longer than necessary. Only when the final pailful has
been poured into the bath do I remove my undergarments.
I stand for some moments in the middle of the room for
I suspect that Mrs MacLeod likes me to do so. Her back is
turned but I can tell by the angle of her neck that she is
looking at me like a hen espying a kernel of grain.

The water is warm and despite my protestations I find
it pleasurable. Mrs MacLeod hands me the cloth and the
bar of soap. I make a lather under my oxters and on my
chest, which is thick with dark wiry hair. My cock
protrudes from the water like a cormorant's head from
the sound.

And what do you intend to do with that, Malcolm
MacPhee? Mrs MacLeod asks.

I reply that I do not intend to do anything with it.

You could put someone's eye out, she says.

Then she takes her little pipe from the pocket of her apron and steps outside.

It is still light and the portion of sky I can see through the doorway is orange above the contours of Lochdhar. I take care of the business in hand and my member recedes beneath the water.

When I have finished, I step out of the bath and call out to Mrs MacLeod.

She inspects me as I dry myself and when she is satisfied that I have done a thorough job she hands me the clean clothing she has brought. She then bundles my soiled garments into the sack and takes her leave.

The decision to let Angus go at large belonged to no one in particular but it would not have been taken if Marion had not consented. Our father was by this time quite enfeebled in both body and spirit. He was fit only for the lightest work on the croft and even this he carried out listlessly. He no longer had the strength to wield a cas-chrom, and when later Angus was to say that he had dispatched my father with less trouble than either of the women it was not difficult to believe. He had no fight in him. So it was to me and to Marion that decisions in the household fell and the two of us conspired in taking the easiest course, which was to leave Angus be.

He thinks himself the sun and we the planets that revolve around him, Marion had said. She sometimes had a fine way of putting things and in this phrase she touched on a truth unacknowledged between us. We were all of us guilty of creeping around Angus like hens round a fox.

If he wants to go wandering off it will only be to himself that he does any harm, she went on.

I had my doubts about this but I kept them to myself and neither of us expressed any misgivings about the idea of letting Angus do harm to himself. Aside from anything else, there was work to be done. There were the crops to sow and tend and always the infernal seaware to be gathered.

We had better things to do than constantly stand guard over our brother.

Some days passed without incident. Angus lay abed late into the forenoon and we allowed him to do so. His cot was in the main apartment of the house and if he was awake he would watch the rest of us go about our business with not a prick of conscience. I no longer bothered trying to allot some task to him. It was easier to leave him be than to set him up in defiance of me.

For some days it appeared that this was not only the easiest course but the most effective. In the house Angus was quiet. His incessant cursing abated if it did not cease altogether. Since he could speak Angus had always been foul-mouthed. It was always arse-this arse-that arse-the-next-thing but since his return from Lochdhar his speech had been little more than a series of oaths piled one upon the other and lacking any discernible logic. Now he restricted himself to calling our father the Arse or the Arse of Arses or the Lord of the Arses, all of which the old man bore with indifference.

If I returned in the evening from the shore and Angus was not about the house I felt a sense of relief. He put us all on edge and in his absence we breathed more freely and ate our meals in an atmosphere approaching good humour. I sometimes wondered where Angus took himself but if he was up to mischief elsewhere I preferred not to know. I suspect that Marion had similar thoughts but we never spoke of it. I confess that if some accident had befallen Angus at this time I would not have mourned him. Nor do I think would any member of our family.

On a certain evening ten days or so after Angus's return from Lochdhar I was outside taking a pipe and saw MacSween on the shore path with a second man who I did not at that distance recognise. It was a warm evening with no breath of a wind. The sound was still and I could hear only the cries of gulls and corncrakes. On such evenings it is possible for a man to feel at peace and for some minutes I had done so. It was only when MacSween and his companion turned off the track that it became clear he intended to call on us. MacSween saw me and raised his hand. I returned the gesture. MacSween is the Ground Officer in these parts but a decent enough fellow and not given to interfering needlessly in other folk's business. If you have an illicit still or have one or two sheep over what is allowed he is not one for running to the factor but will only let it be known you should be careful that such things do not come to the attention of the powers-that-be. On account of this way of managing things he is not as resented as others in his position but still a visit from the birleyman is never welcome. As he approached the house I fancied he must be bringing news of Angus. Perhaps he had fallen in a lochan and drowned or taken a fit and dashed his brains out on a rock.

MacSween, I said by way of greeting. What brings you this way?

A wee bit of business, he said. You remember Mr MacDonald?

This MacDonald was Inspector of the Poor for our island and the neighbouring ones to the north and south. He was as far as I knew neither richer nor poorer than the rest of us but in the few dealings I had had with him I had come to the conclusion that I did not like him. He wore a frock coat and held his head at an angle as if he was a gentleman.

We went inside. Father was at the whisky. Mother was snoring on the settle. Marion was sweeping the floor. John was elsewhere.

Father looked up when we entered. MacSween, he said. It's yourself.

Aye, it is, said MacSween.

And who would you be? Father said, addressing himself to MacDonald.

I am MacDonald, he said with no further explanation.

On account of his position, MacDonald thought himself better than the rest of us and maybe he was. Certainly no frock coats have ever been worn in the MacPhee household and if I owned such a garment I might think myself superior as well. If my father made out that he did not know him it was likely that he wanted to take him down a peg, to show that he was of no consequence to him. My father did not care for authority and he could be sly. Nonetheless he offered the men a dram for they were visitors and when you have visitors you offer them a dram whether they are welcome or not. He did not offer me one but I took the bottle from him and poured myself a measure. Marion put aside her broom and sat down next to me. I passed her the bottle.

When we were settled around the table and had taken a drink MacSween addressed himself to me.

Your brother is becoming a menace, he said.

He has not been himself these last days, I said.

Whether he is not himself or some other self he is a menace.

I see no harm in him, I said. This was not true but I felt obliged to take the part of my kin.

Well, you are alone in that view, said MacSween. Do you know where he is now?

I replied that I did not.

He is at my house, said MacSween. Shackled.

Shackled?

It took three of us to subdue him. MacLeod, Munro and myself. If I can say one thing for him, he's strong. He's got the Devil's fight in him.

He's a wild one all right, I said. But there's no harm in him.

No harm? he said. This afternoon he crept up on my daughter on the rig and made a grab for her. She struggled free and ran off. He had a cock like a broom handle on him.

I was silent. There was no point questioning the testimony of the girl. Since an early age Angus has had a sort of mania for his private parts. As a boy he could not keep his hands out of his breeches no matter how frequently and violently our mother rapped his knuckles with a spurtle or whatever else was to hand. But as with much in life the more one is exposed to something the more tolerable it becomes and in the end we became inured to Angus poking and frottering at himself and to the accompanying snorts and whinnies he emitted.

It was only after a few moments that I noticed a wheezing sound coming from my father's direction. He was laughing.

You find this funny, Mr MacPhee? said MacDonald.

There's no harm in the boy, he said.

My father had always indulged Angus. Let the boy alone, was my father's refrain. When we were younger this caused some resentment but I had come to see that it was not because my father had a special fondness for him but because he was afraid of him. For all his feeble-mindedness he saw that before any of us.

MacSween ignored him.

The question, he said addressing himself to me, is not whether or not Angus is a menace. The question is what is to be done about it.

At this point MacDonald held up his empty glass and I refilled it. He took a swallow and then, tilting his head backwards as if there was an unpleasant odour, began his little speech, all the time glancing at us as if he was a cat about to pounce on a mouse.

It is felt that it would be in the best interests of the community if your brother was confined. He is deemed to be a menace and that it is only a matter of time before he commits some act of violence.

Confined? I said.

To a lunatic asylum.

And where would you find a lunatic asylum round here? I said.

He could be held at the prison in Lochmaddy in the first instance, said MacDonald. Then, if he does not recover his senses, he would be sent to Inverness.

This is claptrap, I said. There's no harm in him.

I saw him not ten days ago strike your sister and attack you yourself, Malcolm, said MacSween.

Aye, I said, but we're family.

This afternoon, if Peggy had not the wherewithal to fight him off, what do you suppose would have happened? said MacSween.

I can't say, I said.

Well, I can, said MacSween. He would have forced himself on her. A girl of fourteen at work in the field.

No, I said, but I could not muster any conviction in it.

He's a menace, Malcolm, said MacSween. To his credit he said it without malice. It was a statement of fact in which he took no pleasure.

MacDonald then spoke again. The consensus is that it is in the interests of the community – and if I may say so in the interests of your family – that Angus be removed.

And what is this consensus you speak of?

Discussions have been had.

What discussions? I said. We have not been party to any discussions. If discussions have been had surely we should have been party to them.

My father had been quietly refilling his own glass and was no longer following the conversation.

We're having a discussion now, said MacDonald. What is your opinion?

My opinion is that you're full of shite.

We were hoping that we could have a civilised discussion, Mr MacPhee, he said. The fact is that there are measures that can be taken to remove Angus but we were hoping that we could reach some kind of agreement. Your brother cannot be allowed to go on terrorising the community.

It struck me then that only a short while before I had been imagining the relief I would have felt if these men had been coming to bring news of Angus's demise.

And if we agreed, what then? I asked.

Of course there would be costs to be borne, said MacDonald.

What do you mean? I asked.

There is his board and lodging to consider.

I laughed. You mean for us to pay to have our brother imprisoned?

He would not be imprisoned. He would be committed at the request of his family.

But we are not requesting his committal, I said. You are.

That is what we are asking you to do, said MacDonald.

I would happily have grabbed him by the lapels of the moth-eaten frock coat but did not do so.

It is not the custom in these parts to bemoan one's lot in life. As long as there is a supply of potatoes, tobacco and whisky a family can subsist, even if the labour involved in the procuring of such necessities is enough to break a man. When asked how things are, one always replies that they are grand. You do not admit to suffering nor want. You act as if there is nothing more a man could want in life than to spend his days dragging seaware from the shore and choking over the burning of it to earn a pittance. To contemplate an existence that does not involve such daily grind only invites despair. It is better not to think of the lavish tables set out before the laird or what pleasures a life elsewhere might hold. When others set off to far-flung corners of the globe, you wish them well and tell them that you want for nothing but the life you have. You call them fools for thinking they can better themselves. They will likely die on the passage or find that they have been sold a lie and spend the rest of their days wishing they were back in Liniclate burning seaware for two shillings a hundredweight. So it does not come easily to admit that one does not have funds but that is what I was forced to do.

MacDonald raised his shoulders and pulled some sort of face. You seem quite comfortable here and you must bring in some money from the kelp, he said.

I felt that his purpose was only to humiliate us but there was no other course than to submit to it.

There is nothing to spare, I said.

I spoke quietly but I do not doubt that MacDonald heard what I said. Nevertheless he asked me to repeat myself.

There is nothing to spare.

I see, he said as if this answer was quite unexpected. He drew his hand over his chin. In that case another solution will have to be found. Do you have an alternative proposal?

I glowered at him. There was a long silence which was broken by MacSween. As I have said, I always thought him a decent enough fellow but I had the impression that everything had been leading up to this, that they had cooked up everything in advance in order that no other course of action would seem possible.

In that case, he said, there is no alternative but for you to take responsibility for your brother and see that he is not allowed to go at large. He must be watched over day and night. If you and your family are unable to do this, more severe measures will have to be taken.

After draining the rest of my father's whisky, a party comprising our visitors, myself, John, who had all the time been loitering outside, and Marion, who would never consent to be excluded from any adventure on the basis of her sex, set out for MacSween's. It was a distance of no more than a mile but on account of the whisky we had drunk our progress was slow.

As we made our way across the moor MacDonald, who as far as I knew had never dirtied his hands in the muck, pontificated about some innovations he had heard of in the management of crofts.

I believe that great improvements in yields can be achieved, he said.

I understood perfectly that he meant his remarks as a criticism of those whose crofts yielded little more than what was sown on them, but John earnestly asked MacDonald about these new methods before turning to me and suggesting that there might be one or two things we could try.

Only an idiot would plant a bushel of grain in order to harvest a bushel of grain, proclaimed MacDonald.

MacSween and I exchanged a look.

I don't suppose you'd pay much heed if I told you how to go about the business of inspecting the poor, I said addressing MacDonald.

On the contrary, said the frock-coated arsehole, being one of the poor yourself, I'm sure you could offer me some useful insights, such as why you choose to live in squalor while still finding money for whisky.

At this I halted and set myself in front of MacDonald, my face a matter of inches from his. We are not poor, I said.

If that were true, MacDonald replied, you would have funds to pay for your brother's committal.

I was grateful then that MacSween pulled me away by the elbow. Instead Marion took my place and offered MacDonald a thrapplesworth of phlegm. As he was a good head taller than she, it did not reach its intended target but lodged itself on the tatty cravat he wore around his neck.

MacDonald did not react, other than to take a handkerchief from his pocket and mop up the gob of mucus. You can be sure I'll be paying you a visit in my official capacity very soon, he said.

MacSween adopted a jovial tone as if all this had been by way of witty repartee. Let's stick to the business in hand, eh? he said.

The rest of the journey was passed in silence.

When we reached MacSween's, MacDonald took his leave of us. MacSween showed us to an outbuilding where Angus was trussed on the ground like a great seal, a thick rope around his arms and torso. His ankles and knees were bound and his hands tied behind his back. The left side of his face was red and swollen and his forehead grazed.

Brother, he said, I'm glad to see you. Look what they've done to me. These thugs set upon me for no reason.

We stood around him like poachers round a wounded stag.

Is that so? I said.

Aye, it's so, said my brother. They beat me without mercy.

I knelt and cut the rope around his ankles with my pocket knife. He did nothing more than waggle his feet a little. Then I cut the rope around his knees. He was quite calm. It took three of us to haul him to his feet. He pleaded with me to cut the rest of the ropes but I refused. We bid good evening to MacSween and led Angus out, myself to the front, Marion and John to the rear. As soon as we were out of sight Angus pleaded with me to cut the remaining ropes. He could not feel his hands.

I told him I was not for cutting any more ropes.

You're a menace, Angus, I said. And you had better change your ways or there will be no ropes being cut.

He protested that he had done nothing wrong and repeated his story about being set upon by MacSween. He's a brute that one. I have a great fear of him.

He then turned his appeals to John who agreed that he had been terribly abused.

At the house we threw him on the cot. I sat on his chest and had John hold his legs while Marion tied him down. He thrashed about fearsomely and a torrent of oaths and threats spewed from his mouth. As with his wheedling tone on the walk home I felt it was all an act he was putting on and there was no truth in any of it. Our mother snored through the whole performance. Father watched from the bench at the table. He had not moved since we had left.

When we were sure Angus was securely tied, I stepped outside and Marion followed. The sun was now low over the horizon and glowed orange. The only sound was that of cursing from within. I took my pipe from the pocket of my waistcoat but it had been snapped in the struggle. Marion retrieved hers from her apron. I filled it from my pouch and we passed it between us wordlessly.

The following evening or perhaps the evening after, MacSween returned. He had with him a pair of handcuffs that had been made by MacRury the blacksmith. He showed them to us. They were crudely made, consisting of two pieces of iron fashioned in the shape of a horseshoe, secured at the open end by a bar.

These are to make sure the boy keeps his hands to himself, he said.

He showed me how to lock and unlock the bar.

I looked at him incredulously. You think Angus will consent to wearing these? I said.

It's not a matter of whether he will consent.

And how do you propose to put them on him?

Is he tied now?

I nodded and we went inside.

I sometimes fancy this house as a skull and myself as the brain contained within it. The two windows are the eyes and the door is the nasal cavity. It is, you understand, a skull half buried in the earth. The thatch is the hair. You might object that a skull has no hair but you would be wrong. The worms dispose of the flesh in short order but they have no taste for the hair. Indeed I have heard that the hair continues to grow after death so my skullhouse with its thatch of hair or hair of thatch is quite credible. There are those who believe that the cure for folk afflicted with the falling sickness is to consume the ground-up bone of a suicide's skull but that is no more than an old wives' tale, or witchery better said. I don't doubt there are some who have tried it but it speaks of a certain kind of lunacy to do so.

From within the house I can see the rig, the shore path, the sound and beyond that towards Lochdhar. The rig I have let go. Why plant a bushel of grain to yield a bushel of grain? The only reason could be to make work for oneself for it is thought that to work is a virtue in itself. But I'm done with all that. There are some around here who cannot bear to be idle. I wonder what it is they are afraid of? That if they lay down their tools for the merest moment they will be overwhelmed by wicked thoughts? That their neighbours will think them depraved? That God will strike them down in the furrows of their rig or that MacGregor will pass by on his pony and see them leaning on their cas-chroms? So they sow their bushel of grain. Not for the yield, for the land here is so poor that a bushel of grain yields no more than a bushel of grain. No, they sow their bushel of grain solely to be thought virtuous. But I could sow a thousand bushels of grain and still not be thought virtuous. For I am not virtuous. It's not that I am wicked, at least I do not think I am. I am neither good nor bad. I simply am. I am a brain contained within my skullhouse. In any case there are potatoes. Potatoes grow plentifully here. You plant one potato and before long you have a dozen. Aside from the planting there's nothing to be done. You put a potato in the ground, wait a while, then you pull them up. You need do nothing more than sit on your arse smoking your pipe. Unless the blight gets them of course. But there is nothing to be done about the blight. If the blight comes, the blight comes. And when the next blight comes that will be the end of me most likely, unless some other malady strikes first. Let other folk busy themselves with work. I am disinclined to it myself. In any case I am not idle. There is always something to occupy me, whether it is the smoking of my pipe or the thinking of thoughts, for a pipe will not smoke itself and the thoughts will not think themselves. There has to be someone to think them. What else is there for a brain to do? If a brain ceases to think thoughts it is no longer worthy of the name. It would be matter like any other matter, like a cowpat or a buttock. The only thing that distinguishes a brain from a buttock is the thinking of thoughts. And in addition to the thinking of the thoughts and the smoking of the pipe, there is the fire to be tended. Just as a brain must be fuelled with thoughts, so must a fire be fuelled with peat or whatever else is to hand. A fire must be nurtured. In previous days this was my mother's job. She never strayed far from the fire, this accounting for her ruddy complexion. Her days were spent prodding and cajoling her fire. She would sit gazing at it for hours, her thighs splayed as if she liked to warm her private parts. She would reprimand the fire if it smoked or spat and murmur endearments when it burned to her satisfaction. The fire was a source of pride. If a neighbour told her, Aye, that's a fine fire you've got going there, Mrs MacPhee, she would nod contentedly. And if any of the rest of us had the gall to take a poker to the fire, we would be loudly admonished to leave well alone. The fire did not need meddling with. She would then spend some minutes poking at it to rectify the damage done by the previous poking. But now I can poke the fire to my heart's content. I have burned most of what was in the house. What use is there for the garments of the dead? I burned all my mother's clothes and all of Marion's. I kept nothing of John's for he was weedy and nothing fitted me. Likewise my father's things. I kept a jacket of Angus's, a pair of his breeches and some underclothes. I still have his boots as he left without them. In fact I am wearing them now. They are better than my own boots but too big so I wear two or three pairs of socks beneath them. Angus had big feet and hands like shovels.

When I am not occupied with the fire I keep my eye on the comings and goings beyond. Folk pass along the shore path regularly on their way to and from Creagorry or Borve. Sometimes they drive cattle or sheep. Now and again they lead a horse and cart. I know them all. MacLeod, MacGregor, MacDonald, MacSween, MacAulay, MacRury, MacPherson, MacLean, MacKeever, MacIsaac, MacAskill, Malone, MacDade, MacCormick, Munro. And once in a while a tinker leads a pony laden with gewgaws to sell door-to-door. They are all of them recognisable, whether by a curiosity of gait or an eccentricity of costume. MacIsaac has his limp. MacAskill swings his arms extravagantly as if swatting flies. MacAulay carries a stick which he shoots out ahead of him at every pace before planting it in the ground ahead of his leading foot. MacKeever wears a greatcoat that reaches to his ankles and swirls about him in the slightest breeze. MacCormick's progress along the path is marked every few steps by breaking into a run. Malone keeps his hands thrust deep into his pockets and his head bent forward as if walking into a gale. Munro has always with him his dog. I don't know what he will do when the dog is gone or what the dog will do when he is gone. Then there are the wives of those mentioned. I know them all too. Mrs MacIsaac never wears a bonnet and her red hair flies wildly about her head. Mrs MacDade has tits so big she looks like she has a basket of peats strapped to her chest. Mrs MacAskill walks at a snail's pace pausing often to gaze out to the sea. Mrs MacCormick has a little skip to her step and wears a coat only in the wildest of weather. Then there are the offspring. These are so numerous I have no idea to whom they belong. Little shits the lot of them. The older boys among these shits sometimes come and press their faces against the eyes of my skullhouse, this to show their mettle. The younger ones loiter on the shore path or venture as far as the foot of the rig. Of course I see them coming these little shits for I am always vigilant, and once they have their faces pressed against the glass I spring from the doorway brandishing a flaughter or whatever else is to hand – for I have no other use for these tools these days – and chase them off shouting elaborate threats in their wake. I'll tear off your buttocks and dry them for peats. I'll cut off your balls and use them as eyes. I'll skin you alive and fashion a waistcoat for myself. I'll bite out your tongues and griddle them with oats. I'll cut off your cocks and shove them up your arses. And so on and so forth. The little shits bolt and once at a safe distance yell some epithets in my direction. To this I respond by hurling stones. I suppose they think me quite mad.

In the darkness, though I cannot see the rooftrees or the walls, the room feels shrunken. I am shrunken myself, constricted in my movements. An unseen hand grips my throat and I am unable to wrest it away. My breath comes in shallow gasps. There is a smell of excrement but it is not animal excrement. It is human excrement. That's something. I can still tell the difference between animal shit and human shit. But are these the depths to which I have sunk? Have I become a beast that befouls itself and lies in its own shit? No wonder Mrs MacLeod makes me bathe.

A week or two after Angus's return from Lochdhar, I took it upon myself to pay a visit to Lachlan MacPherson. I did not ford the sound with any great expectation but one cannot find a remedy for that which one does not know the cause. I found MacPherson in the outbuilding in which he worked. There was a strong smell of animal hide. He was bent over his work and did not hear me enter. I removed my cap to show that I had not come with any ill intentions.

Mr MacPherson, I said.

MacPhee, he said, looking up from his work.

He asked what I wanted.

My brother, I explained, has been quite unwell since his return.

Your brother is an imbecile, he said.

That's as may be, I replied, but until last week he was not a violent imbecile. I wondered if he had met with an accident of some kind while he was in your employ.

MacPherson shook his head. There was no accident I was aware of, he said.

Then perhaps there was an incident of some kind, I said. Something must have occurred to bring about this change in him. He strikes out at all those around him and we have been forced to keep him tied since his return.

MacPherson looked at me. And why would that be any concern of mine? he said.

I am not saying it should be a concern of yours. I only wish to know what happened to him while he was here.

Nothing happened.

Something must have happened, I said.

Why don't you ask your brother?

There is no getting any sense out of him, I said. That's why I have come to ask you.

MacPherson put down the tool he had been using on the little shoe. I don't like your insinuations, MacPhee.

I am not insinuating anything, I said. I only want to know what brought about this change in him.

MacPherson shrugged and returned his attention to his work. He started to tap nails into the sole of a shoe with a tiny hammer. The shoe was a thing of some beauty, bound no doubt for one of the ladies of the estate or further afield in Lochmaddy or beyond. I stepped towards his bench and snatched the hammer from his hand.

You had best not do that, he said.

I don't know what he thought I intended to do and I did not know myself for I had not formulated a plan but as he seemed to expect me to do something I started to bash the little shoe with the hammer. As it was held firmly on the anvil my blows did little damage. I then spied an awl on the work bench. I took that up and stabbed at the shoe until it became tattered. Finally I pulled it from the anvil and stamped on it with the heel of my boot until it was flattened like a bird beneath the wheel of a cart.

MacPherson did not intervene. Perhaps he thought I would set about him with the awl and if he had laid a hand on me maybe I would. I cannot say. At a certain point as I was trampling the shoe I saw the stupidity of my actions but I continued until the heel was broken off and it was entirely obliterated. It was a sad sight and I regretted this petty act of destruction. It had served no purpose other than to make me appear as deranged as my brother. I left without another word and have not returned to Lochdhar since. My mission had achieved nothing besides confirming MacPherson's ill opinion of me.

When Marion was eighteen or nineteen years of age a fellow by the name of Callum MacDade began to come by the house. He was some years older and while not an outright imbecile was somewhat soft in the head. He suffered from no identifiable disfigurement yet there was something curious in his countenance. His head rolled on his shoulders as if it was not properly attached. He had reached the age where it is usual for a man to secure a wife and had set himself to the task of wooing Marion, whom he must have thought was attainable for someone of his meagre attributes. It is usual for those possessed of the finest features – the handsome and the strong – to conjoin with others of their ilk. They then produce offspring who are handsome and strong, who in turn conjoin with others similarly blessed. The less fortunate are left with what scraps they can find – the disfigured or feeble-minded – and through procreation combine the worst characteristics of each parent. Thus the strong reproduce their best qualities while the rest of us become more degraded with each passing generation. Marion was certainly not feeble-minded but nor was she blessed with the sort of features that turns the heads of potential suitors. Her left eye stubbornly refused to follow the lead of her right, her forehead was high and flat, and her nose large and pointed with wide nostrils.

Callum MacDade set about his wooing of Marion by the circuitous route of offering his labour to my father. As we had no money to pay labourers Father turned him away. It was not for money that he offered his labour, Callum MacDade explained, but only to be neighbourly. My father would still not allot him even the smallest task for to do so would be to put him in debt to the MacDades and it is never wise to place oneself under obligation to anyone. Callum MacDade however was not easily discouraged. He returned frequently, saying that he was passing by and had time on his hands. My father became suspicious.

Does your own father not have work for you to do? he would ask.

Everything is in hand, Callum would reply.

He then discovered that Angus was more than happy to allocate work to him and in this way Callum found a pretext to be on our land. He even pretended some friendship with Angus. It soon became clear that Callum MacDade's offers were not born of a selfless desire to assist his neighbours but because he had taken a fancy to Marion. After he had done Angus's bidding for a while he would engage her in conversations I was not party to. Then they began to step out of an evening, taking the shore path towards Creagorry or Borve. They would walk shoulder to shoulder absorbed in dialogue. I cannot imagine what they could have found to talk about as Marion was generally taciturn and MacDade was not skilled in the art of conversation. I took to following them at a distance, this solely for the protection of my sister in the event that MacDade attempted to force himself upon her. This never occurred, at least not to my knowledge, but they took to walking arm in arm and Marion would return from these purposeless excursions with her cheeks flushed and a new lightness in her movements. I was concerned that she was being bespoiled and that no good could come of their relations, for no one would wish to see his sister married off to a mooncalf with no more ambition than to labour gratis on other people's land.

On a particular afternoon he approached the croft and I laid down my tools and greeted him cordially.

What wind blew you this way? I asked in a friendly manner.

Despite the fact that I had never before exchanged a word with him, he did not seem the least bit surprised by my sudden affability.

I only thought there might be some help I could give you, he replied.

As a matter of fact, I said, there is a task I was about to commence that would be greatly eased by a second pair of hands.

I took him to an outbuilding where there was a fearsome tangle of old ropes and shackles. All this, I told him, needs put in order. We set to work together on this futile chore in silence. Then after a while I said to him, I've noticed you have been passing some time with Marion.

Yes, he said, I have taken quite a liking for her.

He was too dull-witted to suspect any subterfuge on my part.

Perhaps then you can help me, I went on. I have lately become concerned about her.

Concerned? he said.

Yes, very concerned, I said gravely. I wonder if you have noticed any change in her these last weeks?

He shook his head and I almost pitied him.

I have noticed that she has taken to going abroad at night.

Going abroad?

Yes, I said. At first I thought that she was sleepwalking but her behaviour when leaving the house seemed to have some intent behind it. I came to suspect that she was engaging in liaisons with some disreputable fellow and while it is not a brother's role to act keeper to his sister, I feared that she would find herself compromised.

The cretin did not understand and I was compelled to be more explicit. I then explained that the situation was more serious than I had first imagined and that I had taken it upon myself to follow her. She walked a mile or so with some purpose in her step and then in a hollow on the moors met with some other young women. I concealed myself in the heather and observed them. What I witnessed profoundly disturbed me.

What was it you saw? the idiot asked.

These women had made a fire which they circled throwing potions and objects into it.

What sort of objects? he said.

I told him that I was too far away to see precisely but that this ritual seemed to agitate them greatly. They joined hands and chanted, then ripped off their chemises and danced wantonly. It was as if, I said, they were possessed by some otherworldly power.

Callum looked at me in horror. Witchery? he said.

I could not say, I replied, for I know nothing of such things but it was a troubling sight and I have since noticed that my sister is disturbed in her behaviour and sometimes mutters things under her breath that I can only imagine to be sacrilege or spells. That is why I wanted to seek your advice. I have observed that you have formed some relations with her and I wanted to ask if you had seen any change in her.

He shook his head but his face had become quite ashen.

After this conversation he ceased calling on Marion. For a time she retreated inside herself and though I took no pleasure in this I knew that I had acted in her interests.

Some time after this however I was forced to reappraise my own actions. I developed a fondness for the daughter of a neighbour. Her name was Peggy MacRury. I believe I was seventeen at this time, Peggy a little older. I know this because we had been in school together though I had paid little heed to her then. Unlike my sister, Peggy was something of a beauty. She had a long face set with green eyes and hair as dark as peat bog. In chapel we MacPhees occupied the pew behind the MacRurys and I made it my business to sit behind Peggy. She smelt of myrtle and when she clasped her hands together in prayer I noticed how her skin was not chafed and scratched like my own. Her fingernails were pink and clean. She took communion with great solemnity, lowering her head before MacGregor, and I felt that there was something weighty in her countenance. As soon as she stepped out of the chapel however she was gregarious and always surrounded by other local girls engaged in gossip and laughter. Her figure was quite womanly and as I lay abed at night I found myself unable to turn my mind from the swell of her dress and the way she set her hip to one side as she related some item of news to her friends. Such thoughts as these sullied Peggy MacRury and I felt shamed by thinking them but it became impossible to sleep without first relieving myself of the stiffness in my underclothes.

One Sunday I noticed a glove fall to the chapel floor from Peggy MacRury's pew. When we resumed our seats I slid my foot forward and pulled it towards me before stuffing it into the pocket of my jacket. At the end of the Mass, Peggy noticed that her glove was missing and the whole MacRury contingent engaged in a lengthy search. Peggy's mother chastised her for her carelessness. The MacRurys were a good deal better off than my own family

– her father was the blacksmith – but not so wealthy that they could easily disregard the loss of a glove. Peggy herself seemed quite distressed and I understood that this object had some value to her.

Outside I separated myself from my own family and took the glove from my pocket. It was made of soft leather and unlike any garment I had touched before. I did not dare to put my own hand inside it – it was in any case far too small – but instead held it to my face. I inhaled the familiar scent of myrtle and a musky smell from the leather itself. I imagined Peggy's hand inside the glove and then her gloved hand inside my undergarments but I did not defile the garment for that had not been my purpose in taking it. As usual Peggy had congregated with her friends and they set off along the track towards the ford. I followed at a distance. The girls negotiated the crossing amid some laughter, holding onto one another for fear of falling in. As they continued along the shore path the gaggle dwindled as each member of the party reached her own house. The MacRurys lived in a fine house towards Borve and as they passed the track leading to my own house, Angus was running amok in the croft birling his arms about him like a giant insect. Peggy and her remaining companions paused to observe him for a few moments before continuing. I could not see Marion. Likely she was inside at her chores. I kept to the shore to ensure that I was not seen and would not be questioned later about where I had been going. By the time they reached

Peggy MacRury's house there were still two other girls in her company. I had not counted on this. It crossed my mind to abandon my scheme and return the glove at a later date but something drove me on. I rejoined the path and as I neared the house I broke into a run. The sound of my feet on the track caused the girls to look in my direction. They parted into a little arc and watched me approach.

I took the glove from my pocket. I found this on the ground outside the chapel, I said. And I thought it must be yours, Peggy MacRury.

I had never spoken to her before and had only ever whispered her name under my breath. Speaking it aloud felt indecent. She looked at me with curiosity.

Is that so, Malcolm MacPhee? she said.

I asserted that it was.

That's strange then because I was wearing my gloves when I entered the chapel and only took them off when I sat down.

Yes, that's right, said one of the other girls, because I remarked on how pretty your gloves were and how soft the leather.

I only know that I found the glove on the track after Mass, I said.

Well, the story you are telling and the story I am telling cannot both be true, can they, Malcolm? And I know that the story I am telling is true, so what then can we make of the story you are telling?

Perhaps you are mistaken in your story, I said.

I am not mistaken, she said.

She is not, said the girl who had testified to remarking on Peggy's gloves in the chapel. She was shorter and more thickset than Peggy but only a little less pretty.

I had put myself in a bind but I did not regret my actions as I had already achieved my aim, which was to engineer a way to engage Peggy MacRury in conversation. She had moreover spoken my name as if we were already acquainted.

Perhaps it is not your glove then, I said.

Peggy had with her a little bag secured to her wrist by a thin leather strap. From this she produced the partner of the glove I was still holding. She put on the first glove, then took the second glove from me and pushed her hand inside it. She flexed her fingers to demonstrate how snugly it fitted.

You see, she said.

I felt the colour rise to my cheeks.

Well, I'm glad to have returned it to you, I said.

If you expect to be thanked for returning that which you have stolen you can think again, Malcolm MacPhee.

I should perhaps have felt some mortification that my subterfuge had been so transparent but I did not feel anything of the sort. I felt pleased with myself for having hatched a plan and having the courage to see it through. Indeed the fact that my deception had been so easily discerned meant that my motive must have been clear. I had stolen her glove in order to present myself to her in a good light and had, without having to humiliate myself by blurting out some sentimental declaration, made my feelings known.

I then drew myself to my full height – I had previously adopted something of the bearing of a supplicant – and said, I am glad to have been of service to you, Peggy.

I then bid them good afternoon.

One of them – I don't believe it was Peggy – called out that I smelt of manure, although that was not the word she used, but I pretended not to hear.

For some days afterwards I congratulated myself on the success of my undertaking. As I lay abed I thought of Peggy and imagined that she must be thinking of me. I pictured her in a white nightdress embroidered with flowers. The MacRurys' house was the finest in the parish. It adjoined Mr MacRury's smithery and boasted a slate roof and chimneys at either gable. I had never been inside but I assumed there must be several apartments and furnishings bought from merchants. There was a large outbuilding in which they kept three horses. Not ponies but horses. I did not think that I needed to take any further action for the time being. Sooner or later our paths would cross again or else Peggy would take it upon herself to contrive a meeting with me. Some weeks passed however and this did not occur. Our only contact was when I stood behind her

at Mass, gazing at the fine curve of her neck. Of course,
I told myself, it was not for a girl like Peggy MacRury to
come calling on an inferior like me. I would not wish to
characterise my family as the lowest of the low – there are
families round here more abject than ours – but it would
be a falsification to say that the MacPhees of Liniclate were
a clan into which folk were beating down the door to wed.
It would have been a humiliation for Peggy MacRury to
present herself at the door of our hovel and enquire about
my whereabouts.

For a time I admired Peggy MacRury for acting as if
nothing meaningful had passed between us. She ignored
me in chapel, and if I raised my hand to her as she passed
me at work on the rig she would not return the gesture.
I told myself that she was only concealing her feelings for
me for some motive of her own. After some weeks
however I came to realise that this was not the case. While
in my mind we were as good as betrothed, to her I was
nothing. Or worse, I was a creature to be avoided or
despised. I had been deluding myself and had persisted in
this misconception in the face of all the evidence to the
contrary. With the dawning of this realisation I felt at first
a sort of rage towards Peggy MacRury. I was of no greater
significance to her than an earthworm. For some days
I entertained thoughts of avenging myself upon her in ways
which I shall not describe here, but this fury dissipated.
Peggy MacRury bore no responsibility for the delusion

I had nurtured. Instead my anger turned upon myself. How idiotically I had behaved. The notion that Peggy MacRury with her shapely figure, untarnished skin and fine leather gloves might have entertained any feelings for me was absurd. It was not she who deserved retribution but me. To this end I devised a series of punishments for myself. I dropped a large stone upon my bare foot, beat my head against the wooden jamb of the door and forced myself to grasp a poker I had heated in the fire for a count of ten. None of this brought any respite however for the pain I felt could not be dispelled by overwhelming it with greater hurt. The pain I felt was not a physical one. And this brings me to the reason for relating this humiliating episode. I realised that Marion must too have felt likewise after I had warded off Callum MacDade with my stupid tale of witchery. The fact that I had secretly been the cause of this shamed me. Yet the knowledge that we now shared a similar kind of pain bound us more closely together than ever.

MacGregor the priest is here. He calls on me once in a while. I'm not sure how often. Certainly less frequently than Mrs MacLeod and without any regularity or pattern. I do not know why he comes. I no longer attend Mass and he has long since given up trying to persuade me to return. Perhaps he wishes only to ascertain if I have expired. I cannot imagine it is for the pleasure of my company though I always give him a dram. MacGregor likes a dram. He keeps a pewter flask in the satchel he carries. Sometimes when he is passing along the shore path on his pony he pauses to rummage in his satchel for his flask and takes a swig before digging his heels into the animal's ribs to urge it onwards. The pony is an ancient bent-backed thing that appears at every step to be on the point of collapse. I suppose it is beneath the dignity of a priest to convey himself by means of his own two feet.

MacGregor's visits follow a certain routine. He tethers his pony and though the door is always open knocks on the jamb and calls my name.

It's yourself, MacGregor, I reply.

He would prefer me to call him Father but does not insist. It sticks in my craw. One father was enough for me and Angus did for that one. He begins by taking a tour of the apartment. If he comes across something on the floor he will pick it up and put it in its proper place. I ask him if he will take a dram and set one on the table for him without waiting for an answer. He sits down and makes a few remarks about the weather or some other inconsequential matter. Then he passes comment on events in the parish. This he does in a manner that suggests I already have knowledge of these goings-on.

It's a hard blow that has struck down MacKeever, he will say.

Aye, a hard blow indeed, I reply.

The Murchison lad is showing great promise, he says.

Is that so? I say.

Very great promise, he repeats.

He then asks about my activities over the preceding days.

There is always something to attend to, I say.

He now, as he always does, enquires about what he calls my state of mind.

This is a question I have difficulty answering. I do not know what state my mind is in or even if it is in a state at all. If he asked about the state of the rig or the thatch on the roof, I would have no trouble answering. But the state of one's mind? A man cannot describe the state of his own mind, for in order to do so he would have to step out of his mind to observe it, and a man cannot step outside his own mind because the man is the mind and the mind is the man. They are not like the white and yolk of an egg. They cannot be separated. But I fear that if I answer to this effect MacGregor will take this as a sign that I am already out of my mind, which I am not.

My state of mind? I reply. I thought you were concerned only with the state of my soul.

MacGregor gives a little laugh. I've long since given up on that, he says. But it is not easy to be alone with your thoughts, especially . . .

He does not finish his sentence but I know what he is alluding to. MacGregor is not in the habit of making reference to the events of the past, if indeed that is what he is doing now. He takes a wee drink as if to demonstrate that there is no special significance to his remark.

I do not think it wise to tell him that I am often not alone with my thoughts, that the deceased members of my family – for I do know them to be deceased – are often present in the house and on the rig. This too would be seen as evidence that my state of mind is not as it should be.

Instead of answering I stare at the surface of the table. It is grooved like the furrows of a rig. Within the grooves are solidified strands of porridge. Sometimes of an evening I amuse myself by running my fingernail along these grooves and turning up the harvest. There is a pleasure to be had in this. And a similar pleasure in afterwards dislodging the debris from beneath one fingernail with another and then rolling the yield between my tongue and the roof of my mouth.

I sometimes wonder if MacGregor knows something about me that he should not know. I mean about something I may or may not have done. It is not a question of whether I have actually done what he believes me to have done but simply that he believes that I have done it. A man of his vocation is not going to make an accusation. He is in the business not of accusations but of confessions. If a man admits to something he is accused of that is of no use to him. No, for a priest, a man has to come out with it off his own back. Of course MacGregor has no end of half-wits queuing up to confess their so-called sins. And the more grievous these sins, the more virtuous these arseholes make themselves in the confessing of them. It's no use just coveting your neighbour's ox. Something much more heinous is required than that. But I have long since given up on confession. I have no use for it, nor for the hollow absolution MacGregor metes out. But perhaps, after all, this is the purpose of his visits. He is waiting me out. He is awaiting my confession. He's a patient one, MacGregor, and canny. But he will not have it. No amount of whisky will loosen my tongue. In any case, I am not saying there is anything to which I need confess. That would be a confession in itself, or an admission at least. But there will be neither. Neither confession nor admission will be forthcoming.

I drink my whisky and pour some more. MacGregor pushes his glass across the table and I fill it to the brim.

I do not entirely confine myself to the house. It ill behoves a man to be too much in the interior. A man who is too much in the interior is no better than a prisoner or an inmate of an asylum. So a man who is neither prisoner nor lunatic must now and then go at large. During the day I rarely venture further than the foot of the rig. The land here is common but even if it is not demarcated by dyke or fence – as mine is not – a rig constitutes a frontier around one's house. Aside from the irksome schoolboys I have mentioned and those visitors I have named, few venture onto my rig and when I stand upon it I feel that I am in my own dominion and that no one can challenge or question me. If I journey further than the shore I am viewed with suspicion by my neighbours. Not for any sins of my own but because the stain of my brother's crimes is not easily washed away. So if I wish to go further afield – to feel that I am not a prisoner confined by the walls of his cell – I do so under cover of darkness. On those nights when I choose to go at large it is for no other reason than to escape the fug that emanates from within. I say choose but that is not the correct word. I do not choose anything. A certain urge besets me and I do not resist. The brain must sometime leave the skullhouse. So I walk or perhaps, truth be told, I scuttle. I fear that in recent years I have developed a stoop. Perhaps this is nothing more than a consequence of age but the terrain here is flat and offers little by way of cover to those whose presence is not welcomed. So at least when in the vicinity of my neighbours I keep close to the ground. But still I take pleasure from the night air on my face. Night air is better than day air. Day air carries the stench of manure and bog. It clings to your skin. Night air is odourless and fresh. So I walk the moors and breathe the good night air. No matter how starless the night I know every bog and tussock and burn on these moors. I know the stones on which one can firmly set one's boot and the spots where one might send a corncrake scuttling from its nest squawking an alarm. The parish of Liniclate is not densely populated. One need not encounter a dwelling if one does not wish to. I do not choose in which direction I go. I simply walk and at a certain point I retrace my steps or describe a loose circle. The dwellings in these parts look more or less alike and it has sometimes happened that at the end of one of my nocturnal excursions I have entered the house of one of my neighbours. It is a powerful thing to move around the apartment of a house while the occupants slumber. I have no ill motives. Aside from a few pieces of discarded food, I do not steal. Now and again for mischief I shift an object – some trinket or other – from one place to another so that the inhabitants might wonder when they wake if it got up in the night and moved of its own accord.

Once I found myself in the MacLeods' house. There in the back chamber I came upon Mrs MacLeod and her husband asleep. It was a warm night and the blankets had been thrown asunder. Mrs MacLeod's nightdress lay loosely around her bosom. I remained in the shadows in the corner of the room for as long as I dared and stole away only when the sky began to lighten. On another occasion I was in the MacIsaacs'. I drank some whisky from a bottle that had been left on the table. I then fell asleep in an armchair far more comfortable than any I had sat in before. When I awoke a small child was staring at me. Mrs MacIsaac was not best pleased and chased me out with a broom. I seem not to be wanted in my neighbours' homes.

Some weeks after Angus's return from Lochdhar, Marion, John and myself were on the shore at the seaware. Angus had been quite calm for some days and we had relaxed our oversight of him. I was perhaps even guilty of believing that whatever malady had afflicted him had run its course. It was a fine clear day. The gathering of seaware is an arduous business but on days such as this there can be a pleasure in it. We worked the three of us mostly in silence but with a certain rhythm, and there was a looseness in my limbs that I had not felt for weeks.

Sometime in the forenoon we heard the chapel bell from across the water at Lochdhar. I cannot say what day it was but as it was not the Sabbath there was no reason for the bell to be tolling. I stopped my work and leant on my pitchfork. The bell was not being rung in a regular fashion but in the lopsided manner of a drunk staggering home from the Creagorry Inn. I thought perhaps that an alarm was being raised for a boat that had run aground but such incidents do not occur on days without a breath of wind. Nor at any point on the horizon was smoke from a fire to be seen. I could not conceive of any other emergency that would precipitate the ringing of the bell and I felt a kind of dread that Angus must be involved. I looked at Marion and though we did not exchange a word I knew she had the same thought.

The tide was still low enough to ford the sound and a figure was making his way across the spit of land that most closely links our two islands. As he drew nearer I recognised him as a boy of about fifteen called Murdo MacAulay, who acted as altar boy to Father MacGregor and whose family lived in the vicinity of the chapel. When he saw us he waved his arms above his head to attract our attention. We watched as he approached along the shore. His breeches were soaked to the thighs from the crossing.

Young Murdo was quite breathless when he reached us and evidently excited by the mission that brought him to us.

Father MacGregor sent me to fetch you, he said. It's your brother that is ringing the bell.

Angus? I said. For some reason I felt the need to feign surprise.

Father says he is out of his mind and you must come and bring him away, he said.

I breathed a heavy sigh. There was no alternative but to comply and as the tide was coming in there could be no delay. We set off the four us back across the sound, linking hands against the rising water, Murdo to the fore and myself at the rear. The water reached Marion's waist but we gained the spit without mishap. As we approached the chapel the clanging of the bell grew louder and more frenetic.

A sizeable crowd of mostly womenfolk had gathered at the gates to the churchyard. MacGregor was waiting for us at the entrance with two other men. I did not recognise one of them, but the second was the father of Murdo MacAulay who was also called Murdo. He was known as Murdo Stone as he was rarely heard to speak. Certainly I had never heard him say a word. He was not dumb nor to my knowledge feeble-minded. He simply chose not to speak and for this reason I respected him. It is mostly through the nonsense they talk that men reveal their stupidity. In keeping with his character Murdo Stone said nothing by way of greeting, instead acknowledging our arrival with an upward motion of his head.

MacGregor said, It's good that you are here.

Clearly he was not in a good temper.

I hear that it is Angus that is ringing the bell, I said.

He is quite possessed, said the priest. I have implored him to stop but he abused and threatened me in the most violent terms.

He spoke angrily as if the fault somehow lay with myself.

I entered the chapel with Marion, John and the rest of them in my wake.

Angus had wrapped the bell-pull around his chest and was pulling on it with such fervour that his feet left the ground. He seemed quite deranged. I stepped into his line of vision but he continued without pause.

What's all this, Angus? I said in a gentle tone. It is not the Sabbath and you have no business ringing the bell in any case.

He ignored me and if anything became more frenzied. There was a wild look in his eye. I held out my hand towards him but he twisted away and lifted his feet from the flagstones so that he began to swing around. I was fearful that he might bring the bell, which was of considerable size, crashing down upon us.

I made the gentle sound with my lips that I might use when approaching a milch cow. He lashed out towards me with his legs and I retreated.

You see, said MacGregor. He is quite out of his mind.

I could not disagree.

Young Murdo and one of the other fellows were sent to fetch ropes and the rest of us stepped outside. The crowd outside had swelled in size and drawn closer to the door of the chapel.

It's the lunatic MacPhee, the priest told them.

Aye, he's a lunatic all right, said an ancient crone. And a menace.

He has not been well these last weeks, I said, feeling obliged to speak up on my brother's behalf.

I would have smoked a pipe but my tobacco had been soaked in the crossing and I did not wish to ask the priest if he could spare some.

By and by the two men returned with a quantity of rope. We formulated a plan and went back inside. One of the men grabbed Angus round the legs while I put my arms around his shoulders. John attempted to wrap a length of rope around his ankles, taking a boot to the face for his trouble. MacGregor blethered about the desecration of the Lord's house. Eventually Angus's ankles were bound, leaving him suspended by the bell-pull. I pinned his arms behind his back and the rope was wrenched from him. At this point Angus fell to the stone floor cursing. Three of us sat on him and he was trussed up. We let him thrash about until he had spent his energy. A hand-cart was brought and we carried him to the door and threw him onto it, amid much laughter from the onlookers. We then trundled him to the shore, but the tide was now such that it was impossible to ford the sound. Murdo Stone went off to fetch a boat.

Angus was hauled once again to the boat, quieter now. Marion sat at the bow, John at the stern and I took the oars, my arse inches from my brother's face which had been bloodied in the struggle. I do not know if anyone had purposefully struck him but I cannot say he would not have deserved it. The Lochdhar contingent pushed us off and I pulled some good strokes to put some distance between us and them. I then shipped the oars and let us drift for some minutes. If the weather had been less clement and the boat capsized, our troubles with Angus would have been swiftly over but the breeze barely rippled the surface of the water. It struck me as I took up the oars again that the entire issue of my mother's womb was contained in that small vessel. It would take only a sudden swell to put an end to us all. Among families concerned with the fishing a whole generation could be lost like that, but we MacPhees were like limpets clinging stubbornly to the land. It crossed my mind as we neared the shore that were I to deliberately overturn the boat, the three of would likely make it to safety while Angus, shackled as he was, would perish. For a moment my eyes locked with Marion's and I wondered if she was having the same thought. Perhaps she was even imploring me to act but there was no reason that it should not be she to capsize the boat. I gave her a look which was intended to convey this thought but neither of us acted.

Neither that evening nor at any later time did I ask Angus why he had gone to the chapel to ring the bell. It was not that I restrained myself from doing so. The question simply did not occur to me. We MacPhees had never concerned ourselves much with the why of things. We were folk who accepted things as they were. Most likely it made little sense for us to gather seaware to burn it for kelp but we did not question it.

But now, as I relate this incident, I have cause to wonder why Angus rang the bell. If he had tripped and cracked his skull on a rock I would not have wondered why he had done so. It would have been nothing more than an accident, an event without meaning. But this was not an accident. It was a purposeful act. In order to ring the bell Angus had first to ford the sound, make his way to the

chapel and then secure the bell-pull around his chest.
Even in his troubled state of mind, he must have had some
reason for doing so. If any other person – even a dimwit
like John – had rung the bell I would have asked him why
he had done so. But because we viewed Angus as a lunatic,
we saw his deed as no more than an act of madness and
thus empty of meaning. But whether a bell is being rung by
a lunatic or a person of sound mind, the act is the same.
And the meaning of the act is the same. It can only be to
raise an alarm. It may be that Angus's act was nothing
more than buffoonery, just as when as an infant he had run
amok in the schoolroom. But when I think about it now
years distant, I believe that Angus wanted to warn us of
something – mostly likely of what he did not know himself
– but we none of us paid any heed. My only thoughts at the
time were of the humiliation that Angus was heaping upon
our family and my increasing loathing of him.

A week must have passed as Mrs MacLeod is here. There will be no bath today as even if I am mistaken in my belief that she makes me bathe once a month I am certain that she has never made me bathe on two consecutive visits. Still I am glad she is here. She has brought me some broth which she heated over the fire and which I am now eating at the table while I watch her go about her chores. I keep the place in a mess so she has something to do while she is here. If she did not think me helpless, what reason would she have to come? Sometimes she chastises me for the boorach I live in but she does so in a cheerful way. Malcolm, she will say, I sometimes think you are no better than a pig in a sty. And I will oink like a pig to amuse her. She has her back to me now but she is talking about one of her sons. He has been kicked on the head by a horse and has lain abed this last week. The doctor had to be summoned from Lochmaddy but the boy is now recovering.

I am glad to hear it. He's a fine young lad, I say although I have no idea which of the little shits that yell insults at me he is.

Yes, we have great hopes for him, she says.

Her apron is tied around her waist and this exalts the shape of her behind. She must know that I have never

known a woman or at least that I have not known a woman
for a very long time, and yet she does not appear afraid that
I will force myself upon her. She is no weakling but there
is no question that she would be strong enough to fend me
off were I to do so. It would be a simple enough matter to
overpower her. I cannot pretend that I have not thought of
it, indeed that I do not think of it on a weekly basis or even
more often than that. But just because one has a thought
does not mean that one must act on that thought. One
cannot choose what thoughts one has but one can choose
whether to act upon them. That is what distinguishes us
from beasts. But certainly there can be no act without
there first having been a thought. The thought is the seed
of the act but not all seeds germinate. Some fall on stony
ground or are eaten by birds or trampled underfoot. So it
does not follow that just because from time to time I think
about forcing myself on Mrs MacLeod then at some point
I will commit this act. This is evidenced by the fact that I
have been having such thoughts about Mrs MacLeod for a
long time and have never yet done so. What is it that
deters me? One thing I can tell you is that it is not
MacGregor's blathering about sin, mortal or otherwise.
Such considerations do not enter my head for if there is a
hell, that is where I am destined regardless of how I behave
towards Mrs MacLeod or anyone else. Indeed the certainty
of damnation is a spur to act upon one's most wicked
thoughts, for if one is already condemned what reason is

there to exercise restraint? Instead what checks me is that I do not wish to be like my brother. Angus was a creature incapable of restraint. Everything spilled out of him, whether the curses from his mouth, the farts from his arse or the ejaculate from his cock. He was no better than an animal and it is a commonly held view that I am no better. My sole means of countering this ill opinion of me is that I do not force myself on Mrs MacLeod. I sometimes even fancy that this is why she calls on me. I could after all survive quite adequately without her. What reason is there for a solitary man to take a bath? If I stink there is none but my own nose to offend and I confess that I find the odours that emanate from the crevices of my body quite agreeable. My cleanliness can be of no concern to Mrs MacLeod, and that being the case I can only surmise that her visits here have no other purpose than to offer me the opportunity of exercising restraint, to demonstrate that despite my ragged clothing, frequent state of inebriation and the dilapidated condition of my hovel, I am still a man and moreover a man capable of behaving in a civilised manner towards his neighbour's wife. The second reason is simpler. If I were to force myself on Mrs MacLeod she would think ill of me, and that is something I could not bear. Do not think that I am deluded enough to imagine that Mrs MacLeod harbours some fond thoughts about me or secretly wishes for me to force myself upon her. I believe no such thing. It is enough that she tolerates me and were she to cease her visits or send someone else in her stead my existence would become intolerable.

In any case, can it really be so different to ejaculate into the soft parts of a woman than to do so into one's hand? When, on occasion, I have chanced upon a couple engaged in copulation and have availed myself of the opportunity to observe them, there seems little pleasure in it for either party. The female generally wears an expression of concentration as if she is performing a complicated feat of mental arithmetic, while the male is reduced to a grunting, convulsive beast. I would no more wish to replicate such a state than I would to trade places with a madman seized by a fit.

Some days after the tolling of the bell, MacSween and MacGregor arrived in the late afternoon with a man I did not know. My sister and I were occupied with the day's haul. Marion was standing on the cart, forking the seaware to the ground, while I spread it out to dry. We had unharnessed the pony and he was chewing on a tussock of grass.

That's a good lot of seaware you've gathered, said MacSween.

There might be a shilling in it if we're lucky, I said.

A shilling's a shilling.

I leant on my pitching fork. Marion stopped shovelling and observed the gathering of men, her arm raised to shield her eyes against the sun.

The third man did not have the air of a gentleman but neither was he a labourer. He wore a tweed suit with a waistcoat, a collared shirt and a bow tie.

This is Doctor MacLean, said MacSween. He has come from Lochmaddy to see Angus.

Has he now? I said.

The doctor bid me good day in a cordial manner and bowed his head in Marion's direction.

We can't be carrying on like this, said MacSween. It is felt that it is only a matter of time before Angus causes harm to someone. Or to himself.

This business with the bell, MacGregor put in, we can't be putting up with such mischief.

Is that your concern? I said. Your arsing bell?

My concern is for the welfare of the parish, he said. The fingers of his right hand fidgeted with the buttons of his coat. He was wanting the flask he kept in the pocket.

I reminded them that we did not have the funds to meet the costs of Angus's incarceration.

Incarceration is not the word I would use, Mr MacPhee, said the doctor. Your brother would be well cared for and treated for whatever malady has afflicted him. Great strides are being made these days in the treatment of lunacy.

That's as may be, I said, but if there's no money, there's no money. In any case, Angus is much improved these last days.

MacSween then explained that if Angus was officially committed by a medical practitioner, the costs would be met by the parish.

So it was serious then, this visit. They meant one way or another to have Angus locked up.

Marion had climbed down from the cart and was standing next to me. Since you have come all this way, Doctor, she said, it can do no harm for you to examine him.

I wondered in these moments if we might be released once and for all from our great burden, from the strain of constantly worrying about where Angus was or what trouble he might be making, and from the vexation he caused from the moment we woke until the moment we laid down our heads to sleep. He sometimes even came to me in my dreams so that I felt that Angus penetrated my whole being. The prospect of being relieved of this was more intoxicating than any swallow of whisky, but hope is not a welcome visitor in these parts. Hope serves only as a buttress to misery. It is better all round to accept one's lot in life and not entertain notions of a less onerous existence.

It's true that he has been behaving erratically of late, I said.

And where is he, the patient? asked the doctor.

Angus had all afternoon been sitting on a hummock two or three hundred yards from the house, well in sight of where Marion and I had been working. I pointed in his direction, then summoned John to fetch him, calculating that if the whole company set off in his direction he would be sure to take flight. The rest of us went inside. Father was stupefied by whisky. Mother was on her stool by the fire. On account of the presence of the priest she shut her legs but she did not get up. MacSween, MacGregor and I sat on the benches by the table. I poured them whisky. The doctor preferred to remain standing and although he accepted a dram did not drink it. We waited some minutes. No words were exchanged. The doctor took a tour of the apartment, now and again picking up and examining some utensil or ornament before putting it back very precisely in its place.

Marion stood in the threshold looking out. After a

while she said, They're coming.

Angus entered with John at his shoulder. Heavens above! he said. This is quite the gathering. Are we to have a ceilidh? Will you start us with a song, MacSween?

I took it upon myself to explain who MacLean was, but omitted to mention the purpose of his visit. Angus straightened his hair with his hands and walked over to where MacLean was standing.

It's good of you to come all this way, Doctor, he said. It's true that I have not been myself these last few weeks, but I have been feeling somewhat better lately.

MacLean replied that he was pleased to hear that and asked if he would nevertheless consent to being examined.

By all means, Angus replied. He then glanced at me and winked.

The doctor asked if there was a suitable place to carry out his assessment.

There is only the back chamber where my mother and father sleep, I said.

The back chamber it is then, he said.

Angus went willingly and the doctor made no objection when I followed them and closed the door. The floor was strewn with various garments which I gathered up and pushed into the wooden chest. The doctor directed Angus to sit on the bed and take off his chemise. This he did quite placidly. From the leather bag he was carrying, the doctor took a wooden tube, shaped at one end like a trumpet.

He placed this end on Angus's chest, the other to his ear. He stood listening for some moments, slowly nodded to himself and returned the instrument to his bag. He then turned Angus's head to the light, pulled open the eyelid of his right eye with his thumb and forefinger and stared intently into it. He asked Angus to open his mouth and examined his teeth and gums. Finally he laid his hands on Angus's skull and pressed at various points with his fingertips as if he was playing an accordion. All this seemed to me to be quite beside the point of his visit as it was not Angus's physical condition that was in question but I kept my counsel. Perhaps it was some strategy on the doctor's part.

His physical examination concluded, the doctor pulled up a little stool and sat before his patient. You said, Angus, that you have not been feeling yourself. Can you tell me what you meant?

Well, I'm not quite sure I can explain it, Doctor, said Angus. I can only say that I have felt myself not be myself. I know that a few weeks hence when I came back from some work at a man's house at Lochdhar I was a bit wild.

And what brought that on? said the doctor.

I couldn't rightly say. I suppose something must have happened to me for there is a reason for everything, is there not, but I do not know what it was. I do know that in these last weeks I have been a heavy burden to my family and especially to my brother here, and if they have sent for you to have me taken away, I would not blame them for it.

But now that I am feeling more like my old self I hope I will soon be able to lead a more useful life.

As he made this little speech Angus directed his eyes over the doctor's shoulder to where I was standing with my back to the door.

The doctor nodded earnestly. Now tell me, Angus — and you must answer honestly — have you in these past weeks thought to commit any acts of violence?

The only thoughts of violence I have had have been directed towards myself, for I feel that I am a worthless individual and of no use to anyone and that my family would be better off without me.

I am sure that your family does not feel that way, said the doctor. But you have not had thoughts to injure any other person?

No, sir, I haven't.

And have you heard any voices urging you to violence?

Voices? He shook his head. The only voices I hear are those of my family who treat me far better than I deserve.

A few days ago you crossed the water to the chapel and started to ring the bell there. Can you tell me why you did that?

For the first time, Angus seemed to give the doctor's question proper thought. He turned his face towards the window. I suppose it must have seemed quite mad and I know that that is why you are here, Doctor, to see if I am mad, but I can only say that I felt an urge to do it.

An urge? repeated the doctor.

Yes, said Angus. I did not mean any harm by it.

But you must have meant something by it?

I did not mean anything by it, said Angus. I only know that afterwards I felt the better for having done it.

And will you be ringing the bell again?

Angus laughed, as if the doctor's suggestion was humorous. No, I don't think so. I think I caused enough trouble the first time.

The doctor then swivelled round on his stool and addressed me. Is there anything you would like to add or to say, Mr MacPhee?

Behind him, Angus pulled a face. I remembered how, as an infant, Angus had the ability to worm himself out of any situation with his sly smile. I had rarely loathed him as much as I did at that moment.

I shook my head.

Outside in the apartment, the doctor reported to MacSween and MacGregor that he could find no reason to have Angus committed. There is nothing wrong with him physically, he explained, and he appears quite rational in everything he says. And God knows our asylums are full enough already.

MacSween protested that he could surely not take Angus's answers at face value. The doctor spread his hands and said that he could only make a judgement on the evidence before him.

You might think that the phantoms would come in the dark, during the long nights of winter, but you would be wrong. The phantoms appear in the light of day. It may be that they are there in the dark, but if they are I cannot see them. And if I cannot see them, can they be said to be there? No, they come in the day. There is my father at rest on the rig, tapping the bowl of his pipe on a stone. There is my mother on her stool by the fire. My aunt I see less often for she was less frequently in the house and I never enter her hovel though it is only a few steps from my own. It has gone to ruin. The roof beams have collapsed and the thatch has slid off. But even she now and again sits at the bench gazing at the table as if waiting for her food to be set before her. She was a fat woman who sat with her knees apart like a man and in summer she liked to hitch her skirts above her knees. No one knew how she became so fat as she ate no more than the rest of us. Over time these phantoms have come to disturb me less. A man can get used to anything. I do not attempt to converse with my mother or my aunt. In their lifetimes they were not great talkers and death has made them no more voluble, but I sometimes approach my father on the rig for despite his failings he was an agreeable man. I ask him how the spuds are coming along or if he saw the tinker or MacSween pass by. Of course he never replies for the dead cannot speak but that does not deter me from engaging in dialogue with him. I simply pause after each of my remarks and imagine what he might say in reply. No sign of blight this year, I say in his stead, or, Aye, I saw that arsehole – my father always had an antipathy for MacSween – you'd think he was the laird himself, the airs he puts on. There is no greater crime in these parts than having airs. Buying oneself a new cap is enough to invite scorn.

If I call these apparitions phantoms it is because I am aware that my father, mother and aunt are not really there. Though I have never stretched out my hand to test the notion, they have no corporeal existence. They are visions, yet I feel them to be as real as MacGregor, Mrs MacLeod or any other living being. I know very well that they must be conjured by my imagination for they are long in the ground and I have no time for preternatural ideas of ghouls or unchancy beings. And yet they do not appear when I am thinking of them. They come unbidden and linger for as long or as short a time as they wish. They never disappear before my eyes but if at a certain point I look away and return my gaze to where they have been, they have vanished.

In this connection darkness is my ally. It is not that it can be said with any certainty that these phantoms are not there in the dark. It can only be said that I cannot see them. And it is also true that though I cannot see them I sometimes feel them to be there. There sometimes comes a creak from the direction of the settle as if my mother is shifting her weight or there is an aroma of tobacco long after I have put down my own pipe. At such times closing one's eyes is no defence for it is already dark and this only bolsters the feeling that these sensations emanate not from without but from within my own head and there is no escape from what is inside your head. And then I have the feeling that my skull has become the house in which I dwell and that I am no longer a man with arms and legs and a torso, but am no more than a brain. A brain contained with a prison cell of bone. I become gripped by a kind of paralysis. It sometimes happens that the elderly lose all capacity to move. They are one moment going about their business and then for no apparent reason they are unable to convey themselves even the shortest distance. Their limbs hang useless. Spittle dribbles from their mouths. Their bowels and bladders evacuate themselves freely. They lose the power of speech yet their eyes dart hither-thither as if they are subject to horrors invisible to those around them. It is as if Death has laid a hand on them and neglected to finish the job. I have known cases in which unfortunate wretches have remained in this state of semi-being for months or years on end. You can only imagine that if they had a working tongue in their mouth, they would cry out for someone to put an end to it. But the paralysis that overtakes me in the night is of a different order. I am not elderly and nor, despite everything, do I wish for death. I still find small pleasures in life. There are the visits of Mrs MacLeod and there are my thoughts about the parts of her body that lie beneath her skirts and bodice. There is tobacco and there is whisky. Yesterday a cat brought me a gift of a half-dead mouse and amused both itself and me by pawing it across the floor, catching it in its claws and tossing it in the air until it was decapitated. I know no more of the thoughts of the cat than I do of Mrs MacLeod or any of my neighbours for that matter but I fancied he was prolonging the life of the mouse for the purpose of entertaining me with his display. It is such things that persuade me that I wish to remain in the realm of the living, and if at certain moments I find myself gripped by torpor I retain for the time being the capacity to throw it off. When one sinks into a bog, one must haul oneself out before the mire thickens around your limbs and draws you under. Such moments are not the time for deliberation. Deliberation is the friend of paralysis. When I feel the paralysis taking hold of me, I direct my thoughts to Mrs MacLeod. I calculate how many days it has been since her last visit and from that how many days it will be until she calls on me again. The accuracy of these calculations is not the point for I have difficulty remembering how many days have passed between one event and the next. The purpose is merely to occupy my mind with something other than my physical situation. Then I try to count how many visits it has been since she has made me bathe and thus how many visits it will be until she makes me bathe again. Of course I am a grown man and perfectly capable of bathing myself. But though I accept in principle that a man must now and then bathe I see little point in it. What does it matter if I want to stew in my own stench? But there is another reason for not bathing myself. If I bathed myself, Mrs MacLeod would have no reason to force me to bathe. So when the occasion arrives and she sets about heating the water and drags the tin bath over to the fire, I affect surprise and protest that I have no need of a bath. Of course she waves away my objections. She has no compunction about telling me I stink. I sometimes even speculate on whether this monthly ritual holds a similar importance to Mrs MacLeod. Though she always turns her back when I disrobe, I wonder if it brings her some pleasure to know that for the moments before I step into the water I am standing naked in the chamber, my member engorged. She could after all submit to my protests and tell me that if I want to wallow in my stench, that is up to me. But she never does. I sometimes even wonder – for I was not being entirely honest before – whether she does not desire me to force myself upon her. Would she resist if I were to do so? I confess that I can think of no greater pleasure than to tear open her bodice and suckle there like an infant and then to raise her skirts and discharge myself into the soft parts of her body. If I did not admit this before it was out of propriety, for I know that you are decent people, but the whisky has a hold of me now and whisky has a habit of getting at the truth. It is these thoughts of Mrs MacLeod and sometimes of Peggy MacRury that stir me from my paralysis and I will not deny there is some pleasure to be had from it. Old MacGregor does not know what he is missing.

At night I often hear the clanking of metal on stone. I cannot account for this. Then there are the voices crying out as if in the throes of death or gripped by agonies of some other sort. But these at least I know cannot be real for there is not a soul within shouting distance of my skullhouse. It is my imagination. I am gratified that I am able to make this assertion, that I am still capable – through the careful weighing of evidence – of distinguishing between reality and illusion. The certainty that the tormented voices I hear are only inside my head convinces me that I remain in possession of my reason. A madman could surely not achieve such clarity of thought.

The ninth of July began perfectly normally. The fact that I know the calendar date is enough to tell you that it did not continue in a routine manner for this is the day that my account has been leading up to. I do not suppose that many among you would have the least interest in the incidents I have thus far related were it not for the fact that they serve as a prelude to violence. When a tale promises bloodshed no one leaves their seat, and you may rest easy that I do not mean to disappoint you.

Our family awoke and went about our ablutions much, I suppose, like any other family, without the need for unnecessary talk. Mother served the porridge which we took at the table. Angus sprawled on the settle in the main apartment while we broke our fast. He did not take any porridge as it was one of his habits to pretend not to be hungry and then demand that our mother feed him at the most inopportune times.

Before Marion and I set off for the shore, I gave Angus some tobacco from my pouch and we shared the first pipe of the day with my father on the bench outside the house. We watched as Marion harnessed the pony.

Why not come to the shore with us? I said to him. We can always use another pair of hands.

I was in the habit of using the mildest tone so as not to provoke him.

Many a happy day I spent at work with the pony, he said. I hope that one day I will be well enough to do so again.

I looked at him. There was nothing to my eye to prevent him from accompanying us but I did not say so. Instead I directed John to keep watch over him and Marion and I set off for the shore. Father would do whatever he could manage on the rig.

Marion and I had been at the seaware for no more than an hour before John joined us. Angus was calm and he thought he would be of better use helping us. I did not argue. There was nothing to portend what was about to happen. The day was all blue and yellow. There are those who claim to see auguries of evil events but I am not among them. If a crow lands on your roof, fools like to proclaim that you will be soon be visited by death. If you repeat a prophecy often enough, sooner or later you will be proved right and find yourself lauded as a seer. No matter that you were right only one time in a hundred. No one remembers the ninety-nine times you were wrong. In any case I saw no crows that morning or none that I recall.

If anything, we were in better spirits than we had been for some time. Since the visit of MacLean, Angus had continued to converse in something approaching a civilised manner and I allowed myself to believe that his performance for the doctor might have been more genuine than I had believed at the time. I even chastised myself for seeing treachery in Angus where none existed. He was not clever enough to pull the wool over the eyes of a man of the medical profession, I told myself. I had begun to think that he was recovering his senses and might start to lead something resembling a useful life. There was no reason to have him incarcerated. The fault lay not with Angus, who through no fault of his own had been afflicted with some sort of malady, but with us, his kin, who saw no more than a burden and inconvenience to ourselves in his suffering.

I shall pass over the middle hours of the day as they were uneventful. We forked the seaware into heaps and then at intervals loaded those onto the cart. We worked through the forenoon then sat in the dunes eating the potatoes we had brought while looking across the sound to Lochdhar. Marion remarked that it was peaceful without the tolling of the bell and I understood that she was making a joke. She was not in the habit of making jokes and it pleased me that she had done so.

I replied by saying that I had no doubt Angus would soon put paid to that and the three of us laughed. We worked through the afternoon until the tide brought an end to gathering any more ware and set off back towards the house. I led the pony and the laden cart and Marion wandered a little in advance. I could see from a distance that there was some activity around our house. A woman named Ishbel MacBeath came running towards us and told us that our aunt was dead. I left the pony where he stood and ran to my aunt's house. There I found her body on the floor between the fireplace and the bed. Her face was very much mangled and there was a great deal of blood where she lay. The table was upset and the objects which had been upon it were strewn across the floor. I stepped outside. Two men were outside our house. These were MacDonald, the Inspector of the Poor, whom I had last seen wiping Marion's phlegm from his cravat, and a taller man who from the evidence of his dress was not from these parts. The stranger was dressed in fine clothes and wore a top hat. I had never before seen a man in a top hat, and it struck me as a silly and impractical garment. I have no doubt that if Angus had been present he would have crept up behind and knocked it from his head. Marion was standing before them and I had the impression that they had prevented her from entering the house.

Who's this? the tall man said to MacDonald when I reached them.

The eldest son, Malcolm, MacDonald replied.

I took umbrage at the fact that the tall man had addressed his question not to myself but to MacDonald. Beneath his coat he wore a waistcoat woven from colourful threads.

And who are you? I said.

This is Mr Briscoe from Inverness, said MacDonald. I was in the process of giving him a tour of the parish.

It was Briscoe who then said, Your father is dead, Mr MacPhee.

I resented the fact that merely by virtue of being from elsewhere this Mr Briscoe saw fit to take charge of the situation and for some reason I felt that his statement was not intended merely to convey this piece of information but was in fact a sort of accusation, as if my father's death was due to some negligence on my part. The antipathy I felt towards this stranger prevented me from expressing any surprise or indeed any other reaction.

Is that so? I replied.

And your aunt as well, said MacDonald.

Yes, I have seen her, I said, as if it was a commonplace occurrence to find a relative with her head bashed in.

And in truth I cannot say that I felt any surprise. I have said that I do not believe in auguries or portents and even less in the second sight that some around here claim, but the moment I saw my aunt's body, I had felt with utter certainty that that would not be the end of it. Clearly she had not dropped dead of natural causes.

I pushed my way between the two men and stepped into the house. Marion followed behind me and they behind her. I do not know where John had got to. Perhaps he was also present but I do not remember. Father's body was on the floor of the main apartment. His face was smashed in although to a lesser extent than my aunt's. Blood issued from his ear and formed a pool soaking into the floor next to his head. His bonnet lay next to that. I realised how rarely I ever saw him without his cap. He

put it on first thing in the morning and did not take it off
until he went abed. Seeing him bare-headed and shrunken
by death, he resembled a child. His foot was at an unnatural
angle and his hands were positioned on either side of his
head, as if he had moved them to protect his face from
whatever blow was to be inflicted. It was a sorry sight.
I knelt down and placed my hand on his chest. His body
was still warm but his heart was not beating. I was sorry
for it. Though I had often bemoaned his feebleness of
body and character, I had liked him. He was an affable man
who was guilty only of wishing to pass his days without
conflict. Had it not been for the presence of this Mr
Briscoe I might have let out a great wail but I did not want
to confirm the idea that we were the savages he clearly
took us for. Instead I got to my feet and said, Aye, he is
dead all right, or words to that effect.

My mother was nowhere in evidence. It did not seem
likely that she had fled the scene, firstly on account of her
girth and secondly because she was loth to leave the house
under any circumstances. In addition to this, if Angus had
taken it into his head to kill my aunt and father – for from
the first moment I had no doubt this was all his doing – it
seemed unlikely that he would spare our mother, as of all
of us it was for she that he had reserved his greatest
antipathy.

I stepped into the bed chamber. At first the room
appeared empty. I then noticed that the chest that usually

sat beneath the window had been dragged across the floor in front of the bed. I pulled it back and saw a foot protruding. I threw off the bedclothes and boards and Mother's body lay there, a cloth thrown over her head. I removed the cloth. Her bonnet was tied beneath her chin but her face had been obliterated. There was nothing left of her features. Had it not been for the fact that she was lying beneath her own bed and wearing her own bonnet, I would not have known her. Briscoe instructed Marion and I to lift the body from where it lay. It was cold and beginning to stiffen. When we had laid her on the floor, the sight of our mother's pulverised face caused Marion to faint. MacDonald fetched a ewer of water and when she revived we led her from the room. There, as if seeing my father's body for the first time, she began to scream. It is a measure of the horror of the scene that it caused Marion to react in this way as she was not one given to histrionics.

We led her outside and we sat down the two of us on the bench. When Mr Briscoe and Mr MacDonald asked who I thought was responsible it did not occur to me to do anything other than utter my brother's name.

One evening we sat down the three of us, Marion, John and myself, to our evening repast. It was summer as we had been all day at the seaware but whether it was one or two years since our family had been reduced in number I cannot say. Perhaps it was even three but I think not. When we had eaten and Marion had cleared away the plates, instead of resuming whatever chores were left to her, she returned to her seat on the bench. John had not moved from his place and I had the sense that something was afoot. I filled my pipe and lit it. Marion filled hers too. She took a few puffs and then said, We have been thinking that it's time we left this place.

It was not the notion of leaving that first irked me but her phrase, We have been thinking.

We? I repeated. And who is this we? Have the pair of you been conspiring behind my back.

John stared at the table.

We have not been conspiring, Malcolm, she said. We have only been talking.

What's the difference? I asked.

We're outcasts, she said. What is there to keep us here?

The kelp, I said.

The kelp! she said with contempt. Then she held up her hands. They were calloused and covered in wounds.

Maybe you want to break your back shovelling seaware for pennies for the rest of your life but I've had my fill of it.

Well, I haven't, I said. And even if I hadn't, I don't know anything else.

You could learn something else.

I made some kind of grunt to convey my scorn for this idea.

I won't be driven out, I said.

Marion adopted a softer tone. You're still young, Malcolm. We all are. Don't you want to find a wife?

What use have I for a wife? I said. I have you.

Even if you have no use for a wife, maybe John would like to find a wife.

John? I said. Who would marry him?

No one round here, that's for sure. No one would marry any of us. Not after . . . She tipped her head to the side to indicate that she was alluding to the events which we never spoke of.

I got up and fetched the whisky and poured us all a measure.

And where is it you propose to go? I said. Creagorry? Lochdhar?

To Skye.

Skye? I said. None of us had ever been further than Lochmaddy and only then once a year if we had livestock to sell.

To Portree.

And what does Portree have that Liniclate does not?

No one knows us in Portree, said Marion. In Portree the name MacPhee is not a curse.

Then John spoke for the first time. I hear there is work to be had there on the fishing.

And what do you know of fishing? I said. You wouldn't last a day. Has Marion being putting thoughts in your thick head?

He looked hurt but I did not regret my words.

He stared at the table for a few moments then drew in his breath and looked me straight in the eye. It's not Liniclate I've had enough of, he said. It's you.

I had never known John to speak to me in this manner, nor to any other person. I felt laughter rise in my gullet but suppressed it.

And what have I ever done? I said mildly.

You're a tyrant and a bully, Malcolm, he said. Since we were infants you've done nothing but ridicule me. I know what you call me behind my back. Dimwit. Cretin. Imbecile. I'm not an imbecile and I'm leaving for Portree. And since you ask, it wasn't Marion that put the thought in my head. It was me that put it in hers. If you want to rot away in this God-forsaken hole, so be it. But you can rot alone.

I leant back on the bench and slowly applauded. It was the longest speech I had ever heard him make.

You're no better than Angus, he said quietly.

At this I reached across the table and grabbed the lapel of his jacket and drew back my fist, but I did not strike him. Doing so would only have proved his point. In any case, Marion sprang between us and I loosened my grip on his collar.

John held my gaze, a look of defiance in his eyes.

I had upset the whisky glasses but Marion did not mop up the spillage. I righted the glasses and poured us all a fresh measure.

And there's your answer to everything, said John. The bottle.

There was a period of silence. I drank my whisky and poured myself another.

And what about you, Marion? I said eventually. Do you plan to whore yourself on the harbourside?

Malcolm, she said quietly, I will find work as a servant. Flora MacAskill is at work in a house there and earns more in a week than all of us do in a month.

I will not have my sister working as a servant, I said.

And what am I to you if not a servant? she said.

You are not a servant to me, I said. You're my sister.

She then embarked on a lengthy speech about the abject state of our existence, the dilapidated hovel we lived in and how we were so shunned that no one would share a pew in the chapel with us. How her back ached constantly and her hands were spoilt from shovelling seaware and taking in washing from our neighbours.

It would be better, she said, to be a whore in Portree than to exist like this.

I then thought to cast doubt on her ability to earn a living as a whore but held my tongue.

Come with us, Malcolm. There is nothing for you here. There nothing for any of us. I have money for the passage for all of us. Don't you wish to be free of all this?

She reached across the table to grasp my hand but I pulled it away.

Never, I said. And you will not go either. He can do what he wants for all the use he is, but you cannot. I will not allow it.

It is not for you to allow or not allow, Malcolm. We are leaving for Lochmaddy in the morning. You can come with us or not as you choose but we are leaving. It's decided.

And that was the end of it. There had never been any persuading Marion to anything. In her own way she was as headstrong as Angus.

I felt a terrible constriction rise in my chest. My throat tightened and my breath came to me in short gasps. I let out a great roar and threw over the table, sending my siblings sprawling to the floor. I remember nothing else of the evening for I emptied a whole bottle of whisky into myself and when I awoke the following morning they were gone.

It was perhaps a week or so after John and Marion departed that MacSween and MacGregor took it upon themselves to call on me. It was early in the evening and I was taking my pipe on the bench outside the house. In these first days of my aloneness, and indeed for some time thereafter, I determined to keep up the daily round of tasks. I was still in thrall to the notion that there was virtue in labour and besides I did not want my neighbours to pity me. If they pity me now, so be it. More likely they do not pity me but despise me. But in those days I still gave some thought to how I might appear in the eyes of others. There I was on the rig diligently pulling up weeds. There I was sweeping the threshold. I even took the pony and cart to the shore to gather seaware though I soon realised that a single pair of hands is not sufficient to make kelping worthwhile. I even forswore the drink for a time though that did not last. Eventually the pony got sold for whisky. I was sorry for it, for I had some fondness for the beast, but the whisky does not buy itself.

In any case it was after a day of toiling on the rig that they came. A little earlier I had seen MacSween pass along the shore path in the direction of Creagorry. He saw me and raised his arm in greeting. I had thought nothing of it. A short while later he returned in the company of MacGregor and they turned off the path towards me.

They greeted me amicably enough.

Your rig is in good order, MacSween said.

Aye, I replied. It is.

MacGregor observed that he had not seen me at Mass that past Sunday.

That would be because I was not there, I said.

He did not pursue the point and I had the impression that he had said this not because he cared one way or another whether I had been at chapel but because he could not let my absence pass unremarked.

It was clear that their visit was not a spur-of-the-moment one and I asked them what their business was. They suggested that we go inside and we did so. The men sat at the table and I poured them some whisky.

After we had drunk, MacSween said, Is Marion not here?

You know very well that she is not, I replied.

He nodded. And she left when?

I did not like being questioned in this way and said so.

But she left with John?

Aye, the pair of them, I said.

And where were they off to?

To Lochmaddy to catch a boat.

To Skye?

So they said.

MacSween was looking at me closely and I asked if there was something on his mind.

I was talking with MacCormick, he said.

MacCormick's an idiot, I said.

MacSween did not dispute this. He returned two or three days ago from some business he had in Skye, he said.

What of it? I said.

He said that he caught the boat from Lochmaddy a week or so hence and he had met John at the pier and then spoken to him on the boat.

If you knew John was at Lochmaddy why did you ask me where he had gone?

MacSween ignored my question.

It was only that MacCormick did not see Marion and John made no mention of her. Apparently he was in something of a black mood and not eager to engage in conversation. It seems strange that if he and Marion left together for Lochmaddy to catch a boat that she was not on it. I wonder how you might account for that.

Why should I account for it? I said. I wasn't there.

You are not concerned that your sister seems to have vanished?

Maybe she was on the boat but MacCormick did not see her.

It's not much of a boat, the Lochmaddy boat, said MacGregor. If Marion had been on it, he would have seen her.

He then pushed his glass across the table and I filled it to the brim. I proffered the bottle to MacSween but he shook his head. I took more for myself.

Perhaps she had a change of heart or found some work

in Lochmaddy, I said.

She has not been seen there. Enquiries have been made.

This phrase struck me as quite sinister but I did not rise to it.

She has not sent word to you of her whereabouts? MacSween went on.

How would she send word?

By letter.

You know fine well we are not writers in this household, I said.

Even so, if she had had a change of heart as you suggest you would have thought she would send word. She could easily have dictated a letter. It has always been noted how close the two of you were. Perhaps you had a falling-out.

And what business would that be of yours? I said. I had already downed my second whisky and felt it warming my temper.

So you did have a falling out then?

I didn't say we had a falling out, I said. I only said it was no business of yours if we had. She decided to leave. There was nothing here for her.

And what is there here for you?

What there's always been.

MacSween then cast his eyes about the room as if to suggest that that wasn't much, and in this he was not wrong.

I ran my thumbnail along a furrow in the table. All I know is that she's gone. And that's all you will know as well. I stood up.

The two men remained seated for some moments. They exchanged a look, the meaning of which was not clear to me, then they stood up and took their leave. At the door, MacGregor said, I will see you at Mass.

I made no answer. I stood in the threshold and watched as they walked back to the shore path. They remained there some minutes in consultation before parting ways, MacSween in the direction of Borve, MacGregor in the direction of Creagorry, where he would no doubt stop at the inn to further slake his thirst.

Sometimes as I lie abed at night staring into the darkness I see Mrs MacLeod, MacGregor, Munro or MacSween every bit as vividly as if I were peering out through the eye of my skullhouse. I know I am only seeing them in my mind's eye, but they seem quite real to me and it causes me to wonder where the difference in seeing and imagining lies. If I see my mother stirring the porridge or poking at her fire, I know that she is not there. My mind is playing games with me. But sometimes if I imagine Mrs MacLeod in the house when she is not, the difference – the truth you might say – is less clear, for sometimes Mrs MacLeod does come, or at least so I believe. But what if she does not come and her visits take place not in my skullhouse but only inside my skull? Does it even matter? It matters because Mrs MacLeod's visits are the sole thing that allows me to believe that I am not entirely wretched. MacGregor's visits do not count. He is a priest and visiting the wretched is part of his daily round, for I am not the only wretched soul in Liniclate. I should say in passing that his belief in whatever God it is, this God that is supposedly everywhere, seems no different to me than the ravings of the lunatic in the asylum, or myself when I see Mother at the porridge. But that is beside the point. Mrs MacLeod's visits make me feel that I still have a place among my fellow men, however tenuous. And if I sometimes doubt that she comes, I need only look to the evidence. There! A bottle has been moved from one place to another. I did not move it. The floor has been swept. I did not sweep it. The tin bath is still in the centre of the floor, the water gone cold but not yet emptied. I did not put it there nor fill it for I would never have a bath of my own accord. Mrs MacLeod was here and did these things not in my mind but in reality. But sometimes as I lie in the darkness and my mind takes it upon itself to turn over these thoughts, it suggests to me that perhaps I did move the bottle, sweep the floor or fill the bath, this only to convince myself that Mrs MacLeod had been here. It is a devious thing my mind and sometimes not my friend, but I do not easily succumb to its schemes. Surely, I argue, I would remember doing so. But you do not remember everything you do, it counters. What do you remember of yesterday or the day before? Was it yesterday or the day before or the day before that MacGregor came? And what do you recall of the conversation you had? And it is true I remember little of these things. But I would remember if I had moved the bottle or swept the floor or filled the bath. But it has succeeded, my mind, in sowing a seed of doubt. A bushel of grain to yield a bushel of grain. And I find myself wondering, when these dialogues run in my mind, whether I am the mind that goads me or I am the mind that reasons with this other mind. And I feel that I am not one man but two men. If I am the brain contained within my skullhouse, then there is another self contained within my skull. Were I to give him a name, I would call him Angus. It is Angus that goads me. It is Angus – long gone from this place though he is – that gives me no peace. There are times I confess when I have been driven to beat my head against the walls of the house to drive him out but that does no good. The only course is to wait for him to exhaust himself or grow bored of taunting me, the way a cat eventually tires of tormenting a mouse. And when the morning light creeps across the threshold, I step outside and find the world still as it was. The tide ebbs and rises. The breeze rustles the grass. Malone, MacGregor, MacAskill or MacSween pass along the shore path and I am certain that they really are passing along the shore path. And I think how often I have heard other men say, I'm in two minds about such and such a thing. It is quite commonplace this being in two minds. I am a man just like other men and they are men just like me.

Needless to say I never give voice to such thoughts to Mrs MacLeod. I fear that she would think I was not in my right mind, if she does not suspect as much already. I am careful to behave like other men. To speak the way they speak and act the way they act for I am still capable of doing so. I enquire about the health of her children for she has a number of those and I refrain from certain habits that I indulge in when alone. If I hear Angus muttering his wicked thoughts in my ear I keep those to myself and if he puts certain depraved propositions to me I do not act upon them.

At first light on the morning after the murders twenty or thirty men of the parish gathered at the foot of the rig. When John and I approached they parted like a burn flowing round a stone. A hush fell over the company. One or two muttered some words of condolence, but they did so without conviction and I sensed that there was a general feeling that we bore some responsibility for what had occurred. I could not blame them. It was undeniable that had some action been taken things would not have turned out as they did, but a man cannot stand guard over his brother every minute of the day and whatever mischief might have been previsioned, Angus's deeds had far surpassed it. The only consolation lay in the fact that it was his own family he had attacked and not that of a neighbour.

Naturally MacSween assumed the mantle of leader. Various sightings of Angus had been reported the previous evening but there had been no appetite to form a party then as the menfolk did not wish to abandon their families when there was a murderous lunatic at large. It was clear from these sightings that he had headed north from Liniclate towards Griminish but after that the reports were vague and contradictory. An elderly woman swore she had seen him enter an outbuilding in the vicinity of Baile nan Cailleach, another had seen a hunched figure scuttling across the moors towards Uiskevagh. All though agreed that he had been barefoot and the consensus was that he could not have travelled any great distance. MacSween and two or three other men had brought guns which they held in the crook of their elbows like gentlemen embarking on a stalk. Munro had his dog and John was dispatched to find some articles of Angus's clothing to give it the scent. He returned only with a pair of socks, which the hound muzzled greedily, slabber running from the sides of its mouth.

Munro expressed the opinion that John and myself should not be allowed to join the party. Who was to say that we would not try to sabotage our brother's capture? MacSween dismissed this view and said that it was up to John and me to decide for ourselves. For my own part I had no wish to remain in the house gazing at the ill-used bodies of my parents. Faced with this hostile band of men I felt a sense of protectiveness towards my brother, despite what he had done, and that my presence might act as a brake on the more hot-headed among them.

It was decided that we would first head north towards Griminish and then divide into three groups. A few men including John were delegated to remain in Liniclate lest Angus for whatever reason decided to return home. These men grumbled at being excluded from the adventure ahead.

We strode across the moors towards Griminish, pausing to question householders and search outbuildings. There was a festal atmosphere among the younger men as if all this were no more than sport. Each of them wished to be the one to run Angus to ground and they outdid each other with boasts of what they would do if they got their hands on him. MacSween was compelled to assert that there was to be no violence other than what might be strictly necessary.

At Griminish we separated. I went east with MacSween, MacAskill, Munro and his boy and another young fellow whose name I did not know. This reduction in number had the effect of dispelling the jocular atmosphere. The further we trudged through the heather and the bogs, the clearer it became that finding Angus would be no easy matter. He could be anywhere. Munro expressed the view that if he had a grain of decency in him he would have done himself in. After an hour or so all talk ceased save for the occasional remark to point out a hut in which Angus might be hiding. As we pushed open each rickety door I expected to see Angus hanging from a rooftree, his bare feet dangling over the contents of his bowels.

As the number of dwellings diminished and I lost count of the lochans we passed and burns we traversed, I almost forgot the purpose of our mission. Then, in the early afternoon, MacAskill spotted Angus on a small island on Loch Langabhat. The distance from the shore was no more than thirty or forty yards. He must have swum or waded out. He saw us and attempted to hide himself among the vegetation but when we called out to him he revealed himself. He gesticulated at us and told us to leave him well alone. MacSween shouted that he should swim back across and that no harm would come to him. Angus shouted that he was not for leaving his island and that he had no reason to do so. He then started throwing stones at us and abusing myself in particular. Munro's son and the young man started to throw stones back at him. Before MacSween was able to stop them, a good-sized rock caught Angus on the side of the head, further enraging him. MacSween berated the young men and they desisted. Munro then suggested sending his dog out to the island to drive Angus off. This struck me as a singularly stupid idea but Munro was convinced it would work and the mutt splashed eagerly into the water. Angus showered it with more stones and it started yelping and turned back.

We allowed some time to pass. Clearly Angus had no means of escape. He paced up and down the island in an agitated fashion, now and again yelling a choice insult at me. After some minutes MacSween took a few steps into the water. He held his gun above his head to show it to Angus and said that if he did not come back onto the land he would be forced to shoot. Angus replied that he could shoot all he liked, he was staying where he was. Then MacSween slowly loaded the gun and discharged it into the air above Angus's head. The report caused a few birds to take to the air and Munro's dog started barking wildly. Angus threw himself to the ground and covered his head with his hands, his bare feet kicking at the stones.

MacSween then discharged a second shot into the air. Angus lay still for some minutes before slowly taking his hands from his head and peering in our direction. He was an abject sight and I was filled with pity and shame. MacSween repeated his promise that if he came ashore no harm would come to him. Angus then got to his feet and waded back across. The water reached no higher than his belly. The men at once wrestled him to the ground and tied his hands behind his back. I watched from a few yards' distance.

Brother, he entreated me, why do you allow them to abuse me? I have done nothing. I only came upon the bodies and took fright. It was a tinker that did it. I saw him enter our house with my father.

No one at this point had accused him of any crime and if there had been any doubt in my mind as to his guilt this statement would have dispelled it.

It was decided that we would take him to the Inn at Creagorry where he could be kept prisoner until the authorities could be summoned.

Munro and his son were in high spirits and would no doubt enjoy recounting their role in Angus's capture for years to come as such incidents were not usual in our corner of the world. Once in a while Munro directed his boot to Angus's arse and told him to enjoy the walk for his next one would be to the gallows.

You will have surmised by now that Mrs MacLeod and Peggy MacRury are one and the same. Of course she has changed. It is true that the passing of time has been kinder to her than to me but years of child-bearing have thickened her hips. Her hair has strands of grey. I do not address Mrs MacLeod as Peggy for I wish to behave in a respectful manner towards her. Besides that, I prefer not to remind her of the incident with the glove which I have already related, though most likely she does not even remember it. I harbour no illusions that it held any significance to her. It was not long after that sorry episode that Peggy MacRury was married to Duncan MacLeod. Duncan MacLeod was the son of the Golden MacLeod, so named on account of his flaxen hair. The Golden MacLeod was a stonemason, and a stonemason will never be short of work for there are always monuments to the dead to be erected. He was also skilled in the carving of the ornaments with which the wealthy like to adorn their dwellings and had schooled his son in this same trade. While the MacLeod family still maintained their rig they had no dependence on it. Around these parts they passed for aristocracy, and like the aristocracy they could be generous to the poor because it was no sacrifice for them to be so. Duncan MacLeod was a handsome fellow into the bargain. It followed that he

would have the pick of the crop of local girls and Peggy
MacRury was the pick of the crop. Such is the order of
things. The best-favoured of both sexes are drawn to one
another while the malformed and gloomy are left with the
malformed and gloomy scraps. I once when we were still
in school picked a fight with Duncan MacLeod for no other
reason than envy. One morning I punched him hard on the
back of the head. When he turned round and saw who had
struck him, he appeared neither surprised nor angry. He
set about me with a weary resignation for even the feeblest
attacks cannot be allowed to go unanswered but as soon as
he had knocked me to the ground he desisted and I felt
aggrieved that he did not think me worthy of a more
thorough battering. There was much talk around the parish
about what wondrous offspring the union between Duncan
MacLeod and Peggy MacRury would produce so it gave
me no small pleasure when their first-born emerged from
her womb with a club foot and cleft palate. I ventured to
think that even my own seed would have served her
better. Other offspring followed – I cannot say how many
– but sadly none shared the deformities of the first.

You might wonder why Mrs MacLeod comes. I sometimes do so myself. Certainly it is not for money for I do
not pay her and in any case the MacLeods have no need of
it. Could it be that she comes out of kindness? That is
possible for she is a virtuous woman and treats me with a
good humour which I repay only with filthy thoughts.

More likely she comes out of pity. Children are wont to administer to injured birds or animals they come across, and perhaps it is thus with Mrs MacLeod. But I am not an injured animal to be nursed back to health and in any case children soon learn that that the kindest thing is not to prolong the life of an injured creature but to put it from its misery at the earliest juncture.

It is also possible that she does not come here of her own volition but instead comes here to keep an eye on me, just as we once kept watch over Angus. I do not imagine that she undertakes this surveillance of her own volition but instead at the behest of those in authority in these parts – that is by MacGregor and MacSween – and that she afterwards provides an account to them of my behaviour and my soundness of mind, just as once Marion and I would report to one another on Angus. He seems calm today, or, He is wild, we must keep him tied. For they all of them take a keen interest in what they call my state of mind and none of them ever fails to enquire about it. Mrs MacLeod is the most cunning in her questioning. How are you? she asks when it is clear that I am in robust health. Well, I can be cunning too, which is why I do not reveal my thoughts to her but answer in a conventional way that I am quite well. I know that they are waiting for some excuse to remove me, but you cannot put a man out of his misery as you can an injured animal. It is not permitted. They are awaiting a pretext to have me incarcerated. They wish to rid Liniclate of the last of the MacPhees for I am a blight on the parish. I sometimes wonder if I should not take things into my own hands and make things easier for them. Things will in any case take their course. A man can only restrain himself for so long. If you put enough pressure on the handle of a tool it will eventually snap.

The cellar of the Creagorry Inn had a sort of cage behind which the landlord kept his supply of spirits. MacKenzie was not best pleased at the prospect of accommodating a murderous lunatic for however short a time but MacSween made it clear he had no choice in the matter. The spirits were moved upstairs and Angus, still tied around his wrists and arms, was shoved behind the metal grate. He struggled against his captors, all the time protesting his innocence. I did not involve myself directly. If I can say one thing for the men of Liniclate, it is this – from the moment Angus had been apprehended not one of them had abused or struck him, or at least no more than was necessary to subdue him. I do not think it was my presence that acted as a brake on them. Rather it was as if the gravity of his acts had created an aura around him. Had he committed some lesser misdemeanour, I have no doubt they would have used it as an excuse to set about him without mercy, but now that he was confined behind bars they looked upon him with a kind of wonderment. Word had been sent to the other parties that Angus had been found, and though there was no reason for them to do so these men gathered at the inn and took turns to go down to the basement to view Angus, as if he was an exhibit in a travelling show. You would think they had never set eyes

upon him before. Now when they emerged into the light
upstairs they commented on his demeanour and the way
he moved or looked back at them. The magnitude of his
deeds had elevated his status. Nevertheless, all agreed that
he had an evil look about him, that they had always seen it
and it had only been a matter of time before something like
this happened.

It was decided that pairs of men should take turns to
stand guard over him until such time as the authorities
arrived to take charge of the situation. I did not recuse
myself from this rotation as I did not wish to appear to
take the side of my brother against the community. Nor,
I confess, did I have any wish to return to a house full of
cadavers. Following some discussion, lots were drawn, the
result of which was that MacSween and myself would keep
watch through the small hours of the night. That mattered
little since no daylight penetrated the cellar. MacKenzie
was in a fearful sulk. How could he open his doors when
he had a madman in the cellar? Nobody paid him any heed.

I took myself away from the company and walked the
short distance to the shore. The sun was shining and the
water of the sound lapped the stones. I could hear the calls
of gulls and from somewhere behind the faint mewing of
sheep. A cormorant dived and emerged then dived and
emerged again. Everything was precisely as it had always
been and yet a mile or so away my mother, father and aunt
were laid out with their heads bashed in. That they had

ceased to exist had no bearing on the world. Everything continued just as it always had. There are men like Napoleon whose names become known far beyond the country of their birth. My father's name was unknown beyond the district of Liniclate and even here he had been of no consequence. The only notable thing about him was the manner of his death. I took out my pipe and filled it from my pouch and lit it. It tasted just as it always had.

Back at the inn, the men were taking full advantage of the cases of spirits that had been removed from the cellar. MacSween had assured the innkeeper that he would be compensated from the parish coffers and this had the effect of dispelling his foul temper. Whisky and ale flowed liberally. There was an atmosphere of revelry and none of the men showed any desire to return to their families. For them, this was a day unlike any other and they wished to mark it by becoming so inebriated that they would have no memory of it. Munro and his son recounted over and over their role in the capture of the maniac and with every telling the violence of the tale and their own heroism grew. By the time night had fallen, Angus was Hercules.

When our turn to watch over Angus came MacSween approached me and indicated with a motion of his head that we should go down. I had by that time taken a good deal of whisky myself. It was possible to descend to the cellar without making oneself visible from behind the metal gate and this I did because we had been told that Angus had been calm for a while and I did not wish my presence to agitate him. Nor did I wish for him to embark on some entreaties to me to free him from his unjust imprisonment. I took a chair and placed it with its back to a wall where I could not be seen. The cellar was lit by a single candle and, despite the mild temperature above, the air was frigid. I pulled the collar of my jacket tight around my neck and set my feet on a crate in front of me. MacSween sat himself on a second chair in front of the grate. There was no sound from within for some time – I could not say for how long – save for the occasional loud exhalations. Then after some shifting around, perhaps Angus manoeuvring himself from a prone to a sitting position, he began to speak.

It's yourself, MacSween, he said.

Aye, it's myself, MacSween replied.

I don't suppose you could do anything about these ties, said Angus.

No, I don't suppose I could.

There was a period of silence. I had the sense that Angus was now standing close to the gate.

It's a terrible thing you have done, Angus, MacSween said.

Well, said Angus, that might be but they had it coming. It was coming. Could you not loosen these ties? They are cutting my wrists.

I saw MacSween shake his head. Then he asked, And how was it they had it coming?

Ach, said Angus. I'd had enough of the lot of them. But it was my mother's fault. Yes, it was all my mother's fault. I was thinking to ready myself to go to the shore to help my brother with the seaware for I've always had an awful fondness for that pony and I asked my mother for some porridge. She said that if I had wanted some porridge I should have had it when the others had it, that she was not about to get up and make porridge for me when it was not the time for making porridge and I said but there is surely still some porridge in the pot and she said that there might be some porridge in the pot but I could not have it because the time for porridge had gone and she was not there to be at the beck and call of an idle good-for-nothing. An idle good-for-nothing she called me. And she who never shifted her arse from the fire. So I told her that she was a good-for-nothing herself for all she did all day was warm her cunt by the fire. And she then said that if I did not mend my tongue she would warm my cunt by the fire which was a stupid thing to say as I do not have a cunt. But my mother is a stupid woman who is wont to say such stupid things and was in general no stranger to abusing me. So I stood up and told her that if she did not get me some porridge I would smash in her head. And she said that if I smashed in her head I would certainly not be getting any porridge. I stepped across the apartment and stood over her and told her that I was only wanting some porridge and that everyone else had had their porridge and she replied

that that was true but that the others had had their porridge
at the proper time and I said, So I am not to get any
porridge, am I? And she answered that if I wanted porridge
I could get it for myself and I said that I wanted her to get
me my porridge. Then she leant forward and took up the
poker to prod at the fire and I took her wrist in my hand
and wrested it from her and struck her a blow on the side
of the head. It was not such a hard blow and she looked at
me with an angry expression and then I remembered that
I had said that if she did not get me some porridge I would
smash in her head. There were some big stones arrayed
around the fire and I took up one of those and then brought
it down on her head. At this she fell off her stool and
I went to where she lay and stood over her. Then I raised
the stone above my head and brought it down on her face.
It was a big stone and her face was quite flattened but I did
it again and then realised she was dead. I had killed her.
You should understand, MacSween, because you're a
decent sort of fellow, that if she had only given me some
porridge like she had given to the others this would not
have happened. She provoked me just as she was always
provoking me even though I have not been myself these
days. I stood looking at her for some time. It was not
something you want to see. I then dragged her body to the
back chamber. I tried first to pull her by the shoulders but
she was heavy so I held her by the ankles and as I dragged
her across the floor her skirts came up around her midriff

and I had to turn away my face for a son does not want to
see what was then displayed to me but I dragged her to the
back chamber and pushed her body under the bed where
my parents sleep. Then I drew across a wooden chest to
conceal her and I thought myself quite a clever fellow for
no one would likely find her there, nor if they did would
they think that it was me that had put her there. I then
stepped back into the apartment and made myself some
porridge for I was hungry and I know fine well how to
make porridge, it was only that my mother had made
porridge for the others and not for me. And I ate the
porridge and left the house. My father was some distance
away on the rig. He is always at the potatoes even though
the potatoes come regardless. You need only plant a
potato and leave it in the ground but he was always at the
potatoes because he had an awful fear of feeling that he was
useless and when he dug up the potatoes it was as if they
had sprung from his own arse and we should all be grateful
to him for shitting potatoes for us. I did not want to speak
to him for I was in a strange temper so I went then to my
aunt's house. She is a stout woman, my aunt, and not one
for the talk but when she saw me at her door she asked me
what it was I was wanting, for I was not in the habit of
calling on her. And I said that I was not feeling myself and
I would be thankful if she would lie with me a little. And
she looked at me and said that she would not lie with me
and I should make myself useful and go to help my brother

and sister on the shore. I said that my siblings did not want my help as they did not like me and that I was not feeling myself and that I would like her to lie with me and have her tit. And then I stepped inside her house which is a very small house which is meant only for sleeping as she generally takes all her meals with us. She said then that she did not want me in her house and I said again that I only wanted to lie with her and have her tit. I then held her by the shoulders and pushed her to the ground and I lay next to her but she was struggling to get away from me and in my pocket I had the handcuff that had been made for me and which I had broken as they were of poor construction and I took it and struck her across the face with it. Her cheek was cut open and blood flowed out but she still tried to squirm away from me. When I was a boy I liked to turn up stones on the shore and under them would be eels that would slither around when exposed and I was put in mind of this. She was now making a fearful racket and I was angry because of her screaming and because she did not want to lie with me so I struck her again with the handcuff and this time she sank back onto the ground and her breath came in short gasps. I then went outside and found a good-sized stone and went back inside and did her to death.

There was then a pause of some duration. MacSween did not say anything.

I lay down next to her for a while as I was out of breath.

Then I got up and covered her body with some bedsheets and went outside. My father was still at the potatoes but I did not go to him. Instead I went and sat on a hummock nearby. It is a hummock I am fond of sitting on because it is dry and you don't get a wet arse sitting there. I sat there for some time and no one would have thought anything amiss for I am often in the habit of sitting there. But as I sat there I realised that at some point my father or one of my siblings would go looking for my aunt or my mother and they would find them dead and they would think that I had done it because even my own family think ill of me. So I thought then that when the bodies were found I would say that when I had been sitting there on my hummock I had seen a tinker call at the house and it must have been the tinker that had done the killing for tinkers are a bad lot and very given to violence. And I thought myself a clever fellow for thinking up this story. Then it came a point when my father made to return to the house and I thought that I should prevent him from going there but he reached the house before me and when I went inside he asked me where my mother was and I replied that I did not know. And he said that it was strange because he had not seen her leave the house and she was not in the habit of leaving the house without good reason and that also the fire was out and my mother never let the fire go out. So I said that she must have gone to my aunt's. Father looked at me and said, Where is your mother, Angus? and I said that I didn't know. Then I said that she was maybe in the bed chamber and my father went into the bed chamber but he did not see her and he came out again and called out her name. Then he saw the blood on the floor by the fire where I had struck my mother and he went into the bed chamber once more and saw her foot protruding from beneath the boards. He asked what I had done and I said that I had not done anything and it must have been a tinker I had seen come to the house and go inside. Father said that he had not seen any tinkers and that if any tinkers had called at the house he would surely have seen them as he had been all day on the rig. I understood that he was right and that I would have to kill him as well so that I could say that they had all been killed by the tinker for then there would be no one to say they had not seen any tinkers about the house. He was in the doorway of the bedchamber and I took up the stone I had used to kill my mother and went over to him and struck him on the head. My father was a feeble man and he went down right away putting his hands across his face. He did not make any sound and I struck again until he was dead.

After a long silence MacSween asked what he did next and Angus said that he took fright at the sight of his father's body and ran away.

Then MacSween asked him why he had done it.

Angus must have been standing right by the grate as I heard some rattling of the metal. He had described everything he had done calmly but he now became agitated.

Haven't you been listening, MacSween? he said. I killed her because she wouldn't give me my porridge. If she had given me my porridge none of it would have happened.

I heard MacSween exhale. I could see his profile in the candlelight. He was slowly nodding his head. Nothing more was said until the next men came to relieve us and at first light some police arrived from Lochmaddy and took Angus away. And that was it. I never set eyes on my brother again.

It is stone cold here but I have not the means to set a fire. I would kill for some whisky but there is no whisky to be had. There is a dim light and I can see the window of my skullhouse but I am unable to convey myself towards it. No matter, I can picture what is outside. There is the rig and beyond it the shore path. Beyond that is the sound and beyond that Lochdhar. Above that the sky stretches upwards. There on the shore path goes Munro with his dog by his feet. There goes MacGregor on his half-dead pony. There is Mrs MacIsaac with her red hair flying wildly about her head and the tinker with his gewgaws to sell door to door.

I see them coming through the eye of my skullhouse. They are approaching from the direction of Borve, the group clustered together so that it is not possible to say how many they number. It is an inclement night, the rain driving off the sound, so it is clear that they are not out to take the air as some folk are wont to do. As they draw nearer I count ten or twelve of them. MacLeod is at the head of them, MacSween to the right of him, Munro to the left. MacSween's gun rests in the crook of his elbow. I have not seen this weapon since the morning we ran Angus to ground. They reach the foot of the rig and pause for a conference. MacSween points here and there and men disperse to various positions around the house. I push the door closed and drag the table against it. I take myself to the back chamber. I'm frightened. There is no question that they want to do harm to me and I do not want to be harmed. I must hide myself. I get under the bed and lie flat on my back. The boards are only inches from my face and I wonder if I am not under the bed at all but in a coffin. I hold my breath.

There is a period of silence.

It is a strange thing, fear. A bodily sensation that begins with a prickling of the skin, then works its way inside you through your stomach, chest, throat and very bones.

It gets a grip of you and the more you struggle against it the more it chokes you. And you realise that the only thing that will bring the choking to an end is the very thing of which you are afraid. And thus you begin to desire it, for whatever it is cannot be worse than the fear itself.

I hear MacLeod calling my name and thumping the door.

Open up, MacPhee, he shouts.

Then MacSween takes a turn.

Open the damn door, Malcom, or we'll break it down.

There is a violent rapping on the door, as if he is striking it with the butt of his gun. I hear the wood crack. It has been rotten for years. I remain where I am for I have given myself no possibility of escape. I regret not calmly waiting for them in the main chamber. This hiding might seem an admission of guilt. Then I feel some viscous liquid on the back of my head. I touch my hand to it and hold my fingers before my eyes. It is black and sticky. My mother is lying beside me. Her face is smashed in as it was when last I saw her. She tries to speak but as her mouth has been obliterated all that is emitted is a fearful sound like someone moaning in terror or vomiting. This then becomes a horrible gagging as if in the effort to speak she is choking on her tongue or drowning in her own expectorations. The men outside have broken down the door and are calling my name. My mother's hand grips my wrist. Someone – I can see his boots – bursts into the back chamber. They are not MacSween's boots. I would have recognised those for they are brown and these are black. Perhaps they are MacLeod's or Munro's for I do not know what colour their boots are. The boots move towards the bed then their owner crouches and lowers his face to the floor. It is MacLeod. His big handsome face is close to mine. He roughly grabs my arm and tries to drag me out. I do not resist but turn my head towards my mother and see that it is not her, but Marion whose hand is upon me. I tell her that I would lie with her a little but she makes no reply. There is a general cacophony of shouting and stamping. Other hands grasp my legs and shoulders. Marion's grip on my wrist is weak and I am pulled out and hauled to my feet. There are five or six men in the room. Having hauled me up they then throw me to the floor and set about me. I do not resist for I have no dispute with them. I do not feel any pain from their blows and do not wish for them to end.

So here I am, wherever here is. A cell or a box of some sort. Perhaps I am already dead, and if that is the case I do not wish it to be otherwise. Certainly it is dark now and I cannot see the walls. Were I able to get up I might be able to feel them with my hands but the paralysis has a hold of me and I cannot shake it off. My arms are clasped around my chest but there is no comfort in this embrace. I do not know how long I have been here and wonder if I was ever in my skullhouse and have not been here all along.

Afterword

The island of Benbecula nestles between North and South Uist in the Scottish Outer Hebrides. It's about seven miles wide, seven miles long and mostly flat. There's a lot of sky and not much landscape. It's not a place that frequently finds itself in the news. In the ninth century it was part of the Kingdom of the Isles under Norwegian rule, before being returned to Scotland under the Treaty of Perth in 1266. Five hundred years later, in 1746, Bonnie Prince Charlie was forced to take refuge there in a storm and was spirited off the island by Flora MacDonald. In 1838, Benbecula was sold along with Barra and the Uists to Sir John Gordon of Cluny who forcibly evicted around 3,000 tenants from his estates before his death in 1858. In 2006, the island passed into community ownership.

The greatest insights into the period in which Angus MacPhee's murders took place are provided by the Statistical Accounts of Scotland, a series of reports compiled by ministers of the Protestant Church of Scotland between 1790 and 1947. While there are no specific reports for Benbecula, which was predominantly Catholic, it seems reasonable to assume that life there was not dissimilar to that on North and South Uist, and the accounts from these neighbouring islands make some reference to Benbecula.

In his 1845 account of life in North Uist, the Reverend Finlay M'Rae writes:

> The people are sober, industrious, sagacious and acute, full of curiosity and exceedingly inquisitive . . . They are insinuating and artful in their address, obliging and peaceable in their dispositions. Those of them in comfortable circumstances are honest; but amongst the poorer and more ignorant, some are addicted to petty theft. It is among this last class alone that this vice and other immoralities more frequently are found.[1]

Unfortunately, he does not elaborate on what these 'other immoralities' may have been. Among the 938 families in his parish he lists: 'Number of fatuous persons, 9; dumb, 2; deaf, 2; deaf and dumb, 1. There are three blind.' He further notes that 'the people have very little money circulating among them [but] to make up for this deficiency, [they] are remarkably attentive and charitable to the poor'.

---

1 *Statistical Accounts of Scotland, Parish of North Uist, County of Inverness, NSA, Vol. XIV, 1845*

He finds that despite the difficulty of paying for schooling, 'the people are anxious to confer the blessing of instruction on their children'. This sentiment is not echoed by M'Rae's colleague in South Uist, the Reverend Roderick MacLean, who writes that 'the people are not, in general, alive to the benefits of education', this being due to the necessity of putting children to work at an early age. 'The poor children are so ragged and destitute of clothes and shoes, that . . . most of them cannot attend school in the winter.'

The overall picture that emerges is one of families subsisting on patches of land too small to sustain them or toiling in the by-that-time barely profitable kelp industry for up to fifteen hours a day. 'The parish is overstocked with people,' MacLean writes with understated brutality, 'and matters must remain in a miserable state, unless the surplus population emigrate, which they cannot do, owing to their poverty.'[2]

Benbecula, or at least those parts dealing directly with the murders committed by Angus MacPhee, is based on material held in the National Records of Scotland in Edinburgh. These documents comprise legal letters

2 *Statistical Accounts of Scotland, Parish of North Uist, County of Inverness, NSA, Vol. XIV, 1845*

exchanged in advance of the trial, held on 6 October 1857, in Inverness; a hand-drawn map of the locale; a drawing of the handcuffs used first to restrain Angus and then as a weapon; statements taken from witnesses; and brief annual assessments of Angus's state of mind during his incarceration at the Criminal Lunatic Department of the General Prison in Perth.

Of greatest interest were the precognition statements. In Scots law precognition is the process of gathering witness testimony in advance of a trial. As records of trials were not routinely kept in those days, these statements constitute the only record of what a witness was expected to say in court. The precognition book in the archive runs to about 130 handwritten pages and includes declarations from MacPhee's siblings, his neighbours and others present when the victims' bodies were discovered. It's important to note that many of the witnesses avow that they cannot read or write. They would have given their evidence in Gaelic, which would then have been translated into English and transcribed by a legal 'writer', so the wording of the statements is formal and often feels heavily paraphrased. The statements are almost entirely focused on the events directly leading up to the murders, and witnesses do not appear to have been questioned much as to Angus's state of mind. But sometimes cracks appear, providing inadvertent moments of insight into the MacPhee family in general and the character of Angus in particular.

The first of these precognition statements is that of Henry Harrison Briscoe, 59, General Superintendent of the Poor in the North of Scotland, who happened to be touring Benbecula on 9 July 1857 in the company of Roderick MacDonald, the local Inspector of the Poor. Briscoe is described elsewhere as 'the very model of a Government official – indefatigable in his work, firm as flint in matters of duty and principle, and kind and courteous to all, the poor pauper equally with the lord of broad acres.'

Briscoe describes entering the single-room dwelling of Mary MacPhee (Angus's aunt) and finding her body around 5 p.m.: 'I saw the face of an aged female mangled and bloody. She appeared to be quite dead but the body was warm . . . I saw enough on the face to account for death – indeed in my opinion no one could be in life with her face mangled in the state in which it was.' Roderick MacDonald remarks to him that she must have been killed by her nephew and that 'he may have committed some other mischief or words to that effect'.

Briscoe then describes going to the MacPhee family house and discovering the bodies of Angus, 70, and Catherine MacPhee, 65, the latter under the bed 'sadly mangled about the face [but still] warm'. He notes that a 'wooden vessel used as a night convenience . . . must have been placed under the bed after the body of the female had been placed there'. The face of Mr MacPhee was 'similarly mangled'.

They return to the house of Mary MacPhee where they find a stone, about a foot long with two patches of blood on it. 'It appeared to me at the time likely to have been used in putting Mary MacPhee to death or rather breaking her scull as she may have been dead before the scull was broken.' Later someone hands him 'a piece of bent iron with two eyes . . . partly covered with wool . . . covered with blood'. This was the set of handcuffs which had been made to restrain Angus and which he had broken the night before.

A search was made for Angus, but abandoned at nightfall.

Roderick MacDonald, 53, largely corroborates Briscoe's account of the discovery of the bodies. In addition, he reports that a few weeks previously he had 'heard a rumour of [Angus] having become insane and that he was tied and then got better', but he made no report of this to the authorities as 'I did not consider myself bound to interfere with him as he was not on the Poor Roll'.

Angus's brother Malcolm begins by stating: 'Since my first recollection of [Angus] he was as sensible as any other person, till 16th of May last. I did not myself observe nor was I told by any other person that there was the slightest symptom of insanity about him.' He reports that when Angus left for a period of employment at the house of

Lachlan MacPherson in Lochdhar, 'he was perfectly well in mind and body'. On his return, however, 'a crowd of people [were] following him . . . he appeared in an excited state. When I met him he struck me and pulled my hair because I would not do something he desired me to do.'

Finding him 'unmanageable', the family keep him tied up, but after some days he is composed and they allow him to 'go at large'. A few days later, the family is visited by James MacSween, the local Ground Officer, who tells them that if they do not take charge of Angus he will be sent to an asylum and the expense of this will fall upon the family. Three weeks prior to the murders, they reported, 'We thought him so much better that we gave up tying him but he was still not sound in his mind and gave occasional violent starts [but] I cannot say that he threatened to kill anyone.' On 6 July Angus escapes, and Malcolm and John find him in a house two miles away. They bring him home and handcuff him. In the morning he appears with his hands at liberty and nothing but his shirt on, but is 'quite peaceable' for the remainder of the day.

On the morning of the murders, while Malcolm is harnessing the horse and cart, Angus is reported to have said, 'Many a happy day I went to work with the red pony and perhaps it may please God that I may be well enough to do that yet.' This is one of the moments when the wording of the documents does not exactly ring true, but there is no reason to disbelieve that Angus expressed this general sentiment. Malcolm instructs his brother John to watch over Angus while he and his sister Marion go to the shore to gather seaware, but John joins them shortly afterwards, saying that he has left Angus at home.

On their return around 5 p.m., Malcolm describes meeting a 'married sister' who tells him that their aunt is dead. He goes to his aunt's house, where he finds her 'very much mangled and covered with blood'. He is then told that his father is dead and describes the injuries he saw and includes the curious remark: 'He was dressed as I had left him, but he had not his bonnet on.'

His account then deviates slightly from that of Briscoe: 'I then looked for my mother's body and found it under the bed. I removed the bedclothes and the boards that formed the bottom of the bed and then my sister and I lifted my mother's body over the side of the bed.' He goes on: 'My mother's body was quite stiff and cold. My father's was somewhat warm. My mother's face was much mangled . . . There was a great deal of blood on the floor of the bedroom. There was a wooden vessel [the chamber pot] under the bed and this vessel must have been removed before the body was put in and then replaced.'

Briscoe claimed that he and MacDonald found Catherine MacPhee's body and makes no mention of Malcolm's presence at this point, but there is nothing sinister in the fact that the accounts differ slightly. Eyewitnesses' recollections of incidents, even dramatic ones like this, are always inconsistent, but the salient facts are not in question. Perhaps as a government official, Briscoe wanted to exaggerate his role in finding the bodies, or just did not think that the presence of the victims' son warranted mention. Certainly it seems unlikely that Malcolm would have invented or misremembered the detail that he and his sister lifted his mother's body from beneath the bed.

Malcolm then reports that he assisted in the washing of the bodies. He appears to have harboured no doubt about who was responsible. 'As my brother Angus had been left at home along with them and there was no trace of him there to be seen anywhere we at once suspected it was he who murdered them.'

Re-examined a few days later, and presumably questioned about Angus's propensity to violence or the motives for the murders, Malcolm adds, 'The only time [Angus] ever struck me besides the night he came home was another night I was trying to get off his clothes . . . I cannot say he showed any particular antipathy to my mother or aunt. Sometimes he would abuse them and sometimes not.'

The account of the younger brother, John, 23, adds little other than the fact that on the morning in question he saw the broken parts of the handcuffs under the bed and left them there. He left Angus sitting with his father on the bench and went to his aunt's house for a drink of milk before joining Malcolm and Marion on the shore.

The account of Marion, 30, is a little more detailed.

'I was the first who returned from the shore . . . but found the house in confusion. The wooden sofa or bench which used to occupy the side of the apartment was out of its place and drawn across the fireplace. There was very little fire and the ashes were scattered over the floor. The remains of two broken bowls were also lying in pieces on the floor. I suspected from these circumstances that something was wrong.'

She runs to her aunt's house, where she finds Mr Briscoe and sees her aunt's body. They return to her parents' house and discover the bodies in the back chamber. Again her presence at the scene is entirely ignored in Briscoe's account.

Understandably, she admits that 'my recollection of this circumstance is somewhat confused', but she does provide some insight into relations within the MacPhee family: 'I think [Angus] had a greater dislike to his aunt and mother than any other member of the family . . . The only people he seemed to have any hatred to were members of his own family.'

This is hardly a statement that speaks to a happy household. The phrase 'had a greater dislike' suggests that he disliked all the members of the family to some degree, and even allowing for the process of translation, the use of the word 'hatred' is striking in this context.

Other witnesses add a few details to the events of 9 July. Roderick MacPherson, 38, a nephew of Angus

Senior, recalls that, as he is making his way to the shore to cut seaware, Angus Junior is sitting outside Mary MacPhee's house 'darning a pair of worsted stockings and doing it quite skilfully'. They exchange a few pleasantries during which Angus tells him, 'I am feeling much better today thank God.' Later, having been shown his uncle's body, MacPherson hurries back to his own house, fearing that Angus might have attacked his own family.

On the same afternoon, a 65-year-old neighbour, Ranald Munro, is returning to his home in the company of Peggy MacDougall, 15. Angus Senior is at work on his potatoes. Munro sees Angus Junior lying face down on a hillock behind the house. He also reports seeing Catherine MacPhee washing some socks at a pool around this time, but this seems unlikely as it contradicts other accounts. Munro admits that he saw her from a distance and he did not have a watch.

Munro also offers some more general remarks: 'I have known [Angus Junior] for 17 years and he always appeared to me as wise and well doing as any in the county till about eight weeks ago when he came home from service quite deranged.' He goes on: 'There was often talk of reporting his state to the Sheriff and Fiscal but there was an aversion generally on the part of the neighbours to resort to this in the hope that he might improve as some members of the family had occasionally fits of insanity.'

It is through phrases like this, passed over without

further elaboration, that a picture emerges of a troubled family.

Angus Junior, Munro reports, comes over to him and asks for some tobacco before inviting him into the house to smoke, an offer Munro declines. As the three reach the potato field, Angus gives Peggy 'a private message'. Peggy herself testifies that Angus called her aside and told her that she need not feel afraid, adding, 'I did not show any symptoms of fright though he said this.' Angus, she says, 'was flushed but he was not more excited than usual'.

The evidence of a small boy, Roderick MacMillan, is chilling. 'I do not know how old I am,' he says, 'perhaps I am eight.' Around noon, Roderick goes to Mary MacPhee's house to borrow a vessel to fill from the well. 'When I was at the well I heard screams from Mary MacPhee's house. The screams were very loud.' He fills the vessel with water and returns to the house. 'On reaching the door I distinctly heard Angus MacPhee speaking in a low tone and Mary MacPhee still screaming aloud. I got quite frightened on hearing Angus MacPhee's voice. I turned away from the door and ran home.' Unfortunately, his parents were on the shore cutting seaware and could not raise an alarm.

Around 3 p.m., Peggy MacAuley, 20, and Mary Ann MacSween are passing the MacPhees' croft. They see Angus Senior at work in the potato field and Angus Junior sitting on a nearby hillock with a pair of stockings, 'striking them against a stone as if he were dusting them'. When they part at the ford to South Uist, Mary Ann MacSween testifies: 'I was looking over my shoulder which I often did being afraid of Angus MacPhee. I saw him get up and walk away. I called out to Peggy to make haste in case MacPhee should go after her.'

Though nothing is made of it in the statements, a clear picture emerges that Angus was a menace to the young women and girls of the parish.

Mary Wilson, 13, testifies that on the same afternoon while she is cutting grass on the moor, she sees Angus coming towards her from the direction of Liniclate: 'He was within a few yards of me before I noticed him. He had no coat on him and no shoes but he had stockings. He was walking at his leisure. I got quite afraid and ran off when I saw him. He followed me but stopt when he came in sight of the house.'

Her mother, Margaret Wilson, says that Mary 'came running to me in apparently great fear'. She puts the time of this incident at around 5 p.m., which, if correct, would mean that this took place after the murders had been committed.

The only further reported sighting of Angus that day occurred much later. William MacPherson, 49, a tenant at Griminish, two miles north of the MacPhees' home in Liniclate, having heard news of the murders and fearing that Angus would come that way, locks the door of his house. 'At 11 o'clock,' he reports, 'there was a knock at the door and as eleven struck the person who was outside struck the door with a switch corresponding to every strike of the clock.'

He sees Angus pass his window with no cap or coat on him.

There are several accounts of the posse which was mustered at first light, and of the eventual running down of Angus to the small island in an unnamed lochan, the throwing of stones, setting of dogs on him and the firing of shots (blanks, according to the statement of Ewan MacLeod, 38).

However, the most perplexing of the precognition statements is that of John MacPherson, 36, a tenant at Balivanich. MacPherson was a member of the search party that apprehended Angus and later took turns to stand guard over him, but the bulk of his testimony is an account of a lengthy confession made by Angus while being held at Creagorry or Gramisdale.[3]

My first reaction on reading this confession was that it was implausible and had likely been fabricated in order to provide corroborating evidence to support a charge of murder. There was, after all, no physical or eyewitness evidence. However, certain details contained in his account seem so peculiar, particularly in relation to the killing of

---

3 There are conflicting accounts of where Angus was held overnight.

Mary MacPhee, that they seem unlikely to be wholly
fictitious.

MacPherson begins by reporting that on the Friday (the
day after the murders) he asked Angus why he had killed
his parents and that Angus responded by saying that he was
'defaming his character' by making such an accusation.
The following day, however, Angus makes an unprompted
confession:

> [Angus] said that he had asked his mother for food and
> she said there was none in the house to give him and that
> there was no meal, but after this that she baked a small
> cake for him and put an egg on the fire for him that he
> only ate a little of it, that she was standing in the door of
> the bedroom and that he jumped to her and gave her a
> blow with his fist in the ear which knocked her down,
> that he stood over her and gave her several blows with
> his fists, that he then got a stone that was to the back of
> the front door and with that he put an end to her life
> . . . He said he dragged her body below one of the beds
> and drew a cog that was under the bed out of the way to
> allow him to do it . . . He then said that Mary MacPhee
> came into the house and asked for his mother and he told
> her that she had gone to look after a couple of sheep or a
> cow or to Donald MacDonald's house, that a little after
> this he went out. Said Mary MacPhee having left the
> house whenever he gave that answer and that he went
> into her house and asked her to go and sleep with him in
> the bed which she refused to do, that he then desired her

to lie down on the floor that she also refused to do that, that he then threw her down and began striking her in the head and face with the said iron [the broken hand-cuff], that she screamed fearfully, that as he was not getting on so rapidly as he wished he got a stone and with that broke her scull, that before then he had dragged her over to the fire place where he wrapped the bedclothes about her, that he then went out and met his father returning from hoeing the potatoes, that his father said that he had been murdering his aunt, that he said he was not and that he had only been calling in, that his father and he went into his father's house who asked for his mother and that he gave him the same answer he formerly gave Mary MacPhee, that his father looked so angry, that he rushed upon him and began striking him with his fists and that he had much less difficulty in killing him than the two women, that after he killed him he dragged him up aside his own bed and placed the chest outside of him, and that he then sculked away.

MacPherson's account of Angus's confession is corroborated by Ewen MacLeod, 38: 'On Saturday [Angus] explained particularly how he had murdered his mother and aunt . . . He said he jumped upon his mother and trampled upon her [. . .] He said that he was desirous that his father and mother should put him in a rage before he attacked them by refusing him something.'

MacLeod further reports that Angus said he washed his shirt and vest and left them by a lake 'with the intention of deceiving those who might be searching for him, and they might think he had gone out on the lake and drowned'.

He concludes: 'I consider him quite mad. He may sometimes say a few sensible words but very rarely. He is always trying to take off his clothes.'

On reinterrogation, MacLeod adds, 'He speaks daily of these murders. He starts the subject himself and seems to boast of having committed them.'

Regardless of the minor inconsistencies and discrepancies in the various statements, a clear picture of what occurred emerges. Some time on the morning in question, Angus killed his mother and hid her body. He then, probably shortly afterwards, killed his aunt. After some intervening hours, during which he was seen by various witnesses, he killed his father and fled the scene.

The legal defence of insanity was established both in English and Scottish courts in 1843 after Daniel M'Naughton, a Scottish woodturner, was found not guilty on grounds of insanity of murdering civil servant Edward Drummond, whom he had mistaken for the Prime Minister Robert Peel.

What came to be known as the M'Naughton Rule states:

> To establish a defence on the ground of insanity, it must
> be clearly proved that, at the time of the committing of

the act, the party accused was labouring under such a defect of reason, from disease of the mind, as not to know the nature and quality of the act he was doing; or if he did know it, that he did not know he was doing what was wrong.

Angus was tried at the Autumn Circuit Court in Inverness on 6 October, defended by John Ferguson MacLennan. As was customary at the time, there is no record of the trial and it merited less than two hundred words, under the headline MURDER BY A MANIAC, in the *Glasgow Courier*: 'The circumstances of this painful case will be fresh in the recollection of the public. The prisoner attacked his relatives, in revenge it was supposed, for having confined him in handcuffs, and murdered them one after another on 9th July last.'

He was found not guilty on grounds of insanity and ordered to be 'confined till the further pleasure of the Court'.

This report was carried pretty much verbatim by a number of newspapers, but that was the extent of the interest in the case. The *Stonehaven Journal* adds the intriguing detail that 'the prisoner . . . said he was the Christ, and that he had the Divine command to commit the murders, and was doing God['s] service'.

Given that under Scots law at the time the defendant could not give evidence at his own trial and that there is no mention in any of the precognition statements of Angus engaging in this sort of talk, this seems at best hearsay.

In any case, Angus was sent to the Criminal Lunatic Department at the General Prison in Perth, where he was held under the care of James Bruce Thomson. Thomson, who died in 1873, was an early authority on the then nascent subject of criminal psychology and the author of two pioneering articles, 'The Hereditary Nature of Crime' and 'The Psychology of Criminals'. He also, incidentally, features as a character in my novel *His Bloody Project*.

Despite exhaustive efforts, I have been unable to locate the records of the early years of Angus's incarceration (1857–73). However, Professor Rab Houston of St Andrews University describes how 'during the first three decades of his incarceration at the Criminal Lunatic Department, Angus was more or less continually deranged, experiencing sudden episodes of violent insanity. During these periods Angus was held in a strait-jacket and anklets. He is also reported to be fixated with his genitals and a "chronic masturbator".'[4]

Despite the fact that alternative forms of entertainment would have been scarce, it seems unlikely that Angus developed this habit on entering the asylum. Indeed, given the evidence that he was a menace to the female population of Liniclate, the handcuffs made by the blacksmith MacRury might well have been designed to prevent this onanistic

---

4 *Prisoners or Patients? Criminal Insanity in Victorian Scotland* exhibition, National Records of Scotland, 2019

behaviour. This might also account for the particular rage Angus is reported to have reserved for these manacles.

This state of violent insanity is consistent with the statement of John MacDonald, the Medical Officer at Lochmaddy Prison, North Uist, where Angus was initially held. 'I have seen Angus MacPhee,' he reports, 'almost daily since his committal to prison. He is quite insane and continues to be in a state of constant maniacal excitement.'

As the decades pass, the annual assessments of Angus's condition grow ever more perfunctory. The first of the surviving reports, written on 29 January 1873, is the longest, and the delusions afflicting Angus exceed anything reported from his life on Benbecula. He had by this time been incarcerated for sixteen years and his condition does not speak well of the therapeutic environment of the General Prison.

> Angus MacPhee has been for a few days rather restless. He does not sleep well and says he is troubled in his mind thinking over his past life. He refers to supposed past injuries inflicted he says by a former attendant. Had an idea that his penis had been injured and is not right and suggested it might be cut off with a chisel and then it would grow in again straight. To have Bromide of Potassium.[5] Strictly watched and excluded from the tool room.

---

5 A substance used as a sedative and anti-convulsant in the nineteenth century.

The following day he is reported to be 'furiously maniacal.
Restrained in jacket and anklets.'

The next update is from November 1876:

> . . . slowly recovering. Has still one hand restrained. Is
> very confused in his ideas and wandering in his talk,
> jumping from one subject of conversation to another
> with the greatest rapidity. It is noticed that every
> succeeding maniacal attack with which he is affected is
> always [of] much longer duration than its predecessor
> . . . Has shown no notice to anyone lately.

A month later, he has been 'relieved from all restraint'.
By mid-1877 he is reported as being 'one of the best and
most constant workers. Still a little confused in his talk but
now very quiet', but the fixation with his genitalia continues.
In June of that year he is said to be 'complaining of enlarge-
ment of one of his testicles (on examination found to be
quite normal) which he says was hurt by a former attendant.'
In October, '[he] says he is in love with one of the female
attendants and thinks that his health is breaking down'.

From this point the assessments of his condition run to
no more than a few words per year: 'No change to note'
(1879); 'Filthy in his habits' (1883); 'Dull and despondent'
(1884); 'He became quite talkative [illegible] then argu-
mentative and dictatorial followed by extreme violent excitement until November when improvement set in' (1888);
'Restless and unsettled most of the year' (1893); 'Has been

more or less dull and [illegible]; kept his bed for a [illegible], thought he was dying of [illegible] and wished to see his [illegible]' (1897).

The final entry in this chronicle of a dismal existence is from December 1899: 'Improved. Had no period of excitement during the year but from time to time became dull and despondent. So fairly rational and works well.'

At this point, after forty-two years in the Criminal Lunatic Department, Angus was transferred to Inverness Prison where he died shortly afterwards at the age of sixty-eight.

Reading through these perfunctory notes, the dominant emotion is one of sadness. Angus MacPhee, for whatever reason, was driven to commit three horrifying acts of violence, but his incarceration, physical restraint and drug-induced torpor can also be seen as acts of violence.

Press reports of the murders themselves were a little more lengthy, but despite being described as 'the most heart-rending spectacle ever witnessed in the Highlands', the incident merited only a single mention in each of the Scottish newspapers. The fullest account was in the *Inverness Courier*, and, aside from details of the murders and Angus's capture, it provides a little insight into the circumstances of the MacPhee family.

The unhappy maniac's father was in comparatively comfortable circumstances, for though his relative Mary MacPhee was on the poors'-roll, he himself was quite independent of parochial relief, and his family . . . were usually well employed on the island. But though the means of the family were adequate to the daily wants of a simple household such as that at Liniclate, it is quite out of the question to suppose that MacPhee could have sent his son to any of the lunatic asylums of the south, and maintained him there at his private charges, and, not being a pauper, the Board of Supervision could not interfere. It is right to add that only ten days before this catastrophe, MacPhee had been examined by Dr MacLean, and he and the priest who ministered to the family considered him unfit for confinement under a Sheriff's warrant.

The MacPhees were poor, but not unusually so. Reading between the lines, however, a picture emerges of a troubled family. I was struck by the fact that the family consisted of four siblings (Marion, Malcolm, Angus and John) in their twenties, none of whom were married.[6] This seems unusual for the time; indeed, the Reverend Finlay M'Rae states that in North Uist 'early marriages have become habitual for ages back'. There is also the

---

6 There is a single mention in Malcolm MacPhee's statement of a 'married sister', but it seems odd that no other mention would be made of this sibling and that a statement would not have been taken from her. It seems more likely that this 'married sister' was actually a niece of Mary MacPhee's who is mentioned elsewhere.

statement of Ranald Munro, a close friend of Angus Senior, that '*some members of the family* had occasionally fits of insanity'. There is the menacing behaviour of Angus towards the young women of the parish, which seems to have predated whatever happened to him at Lochdhar. There is not enough to suggest that the MacPhees were pariahs or outcasts, but there is certainly sufficient evidence to conclude that they were a family who did not have their troubles to seek.

What, finally, are we to make of Angus's great acts of violence? The words 'maniac' and 'maniacal' appear frequently in both the press coverage and in the assessments from Perth Prison. It's a powerful word, maniac: redolent of lack of control, mindlessness and monstrosity. But when we examine Angus's actions on 9 July 1857, they are not entirely the actions of a maniac. While there is monstrousness in the violence he perpetrated, it appears to have been interspersed with a certain degree of calculation.

Even given the discrepancies in reports of the temperatures of the three bodies, it is clear that the two women were killed some hours before Angus Senior. Having killed his mother, Angus did not immediately abscond or go on a rampage. He took the time to hide her body under the bed in the back room of the house, first removing a chamber pot and then replacing it in front of the bed. He also moved a wooden chest to disguise what he had done. These do not seem to me the actions of a 'maniac'. Whether he then went to his aunt's house with the intention of killing her is impossible to say, but having done so, although he made no attempt to move her body, he did cover it with bedclothes, which perhaps suggests some shame or horror at what he had done, or at least a half-hearted attempt to conceal the body. Some five hours later, having killed his father, he finally fled the scene.

He is reported to have stolen a pat of butter from an outbuilding that he then used to wash his shirt, which would presumably have been covered with blood. He allegedly had the idea of leaving his clothes on the shore of a 'lake' in order to lead those searching for him to believe he had drowned. Then, when he was apprehended the following morning, there are his initial denials that he was responsible. While all the evidence regarding his actions in the aftermath of the murders should be treated with a degree of caution, all of it suggests that there was a rationality involved. He did not simply run amok, as the reporting of his crimes suggests.

It is more comforting when confronted with dreadful acts of violence to retreat behind the word 'maniac', but to do so strips such acts of any meaning. It constitutes a refusal to attempt to comprehend what occurred. Angus MacPhee was not a monster. He was a man, driven for reasons we will never know to commit a series of brutal,

transgressive acts, but he was still a man. His life on
Liniclate ended tragically, but there is tragedy too in the
forty-two years of incarceration he endured in the Criminal
Lunatic Department of Perth Prison.

Acknowledgements

I first came across reference to Angus MacPhee's murders in Malcolm Archibald's book *Whisky Wars: Riots and Murder in the 19th-Century Highlands and Islands* (Black and White Publishing, 2013).

My sincere thanks to Jocelyn Grant and the always helpful staff at the National Records of Scotland in Edinburgh, and to the staff at the Mitchell Library in Glasgow.

Deep and heartfelt gratitude is due to James Crawford and Alison Rae at Polygon for their great enthusiasm and sensitive shepherding of this project. My appreciation also to Dan Wells at Biblioasis, Jane Pearson and Michael Heyward at Text Publishing and to my agent Isobel Dixon for their unwavering and invaluable support.

In Darkland Tales, the best modern Scottish authors offer dramatic retellings of stories from the nation's history, myth and legend. These are landmark moments from the past, viewed through a modern lens and alive to modern sensibilities. Each Darkland Tale is sharp, provocative and darkly comic, mining that seam of sedition and psychological drama that has always featured in the best of Scottish literature.

Rizzio Denise Mina

Hex Jenni Fagan

Nothing Left to Fear from Hell Alan Warner

Columba's Bones David Greig

Queen Macbeth Val McDermid

Benbecula Graeme Macrae Burnet